Dangerous Lies

Ella Miles

PROLOGUE
LIESEL

I ALWAYS KNEW that falling in love was dangerous.

I could fall in love with the wrong person.

A monster.

Criminal.

Devil.

A man who could hurt me.

Rape me.

Ruin me.

That was always my biggest fear—that I would fall in love with a man who would hurt me, a man I couldn't escape. That I would love him even when I shouldn't. That my love for him would kill me.

It turns out, I didn't fall for the devil.

I fell for a good, compassionate man. A man with the biggest heart. A man who loves me as his equal. A man who loves my kids as his own.

I found a man who completes my heart—a man I want to spend the rest of my life with and beyond.

But falling in love with him was still dangerous.

And I don't know if we can survive our love.

1

LIESEL

BEEP, beep, beep.

An annoyingly high-pitched sound infiltrates the fog in my brain. I try to open my eyes, but my eyelids are too heavy. My legs feel numb, and my teeth chatter from the chill surging through my body.

Beep, beep, beep.

The sound continues, trying to pull me back to reality. I don't know what happened, but I do know that I don't want to return to reality. Whatever happened was bad. I may not have much of a heart left, but I have to protect it.

Stay asleep; life will be easier if you just sleep.

"Miss Dunn, can you open your eyes for me?" I hear a sweet voice say.

No!

It's a trap. I won't open my eyes.

I feel a hand running through my hair, brushing it out of my face before it lands on my cheek.

"You should open your eyes now. It's time," her voice is still sweet, yet firmer now.

I shake my head gently back and forth. "I'm scared."

Her hand moves down my body until she's gripping my hand. "I know. I'm going to be right here holding your hand the whole time, though. You won't have to face the truth alone."

The truth—that means something terrible did happen. It wasn't supposed to be this way. I wasn't supposed to be asleep when I gave birth. *What happened?*

"Open your eyes, sweetheart. Then we can talk. You still have time to decide."

Decide?

I've already made my decision. Nothing is going to change that.

"On the count of three," she says.

"One."

"Two."

I open my eyes before she gets to three. I don't like doing what I'm told.

"There you are." She smiles, still gripping my hand. "How are you feeling? Do you need more pain medicine?"

"I just need you to cut the crap and tell me what happened."

Her lips thin, and her smile drops, but she nods.

"You gave birth to a beautiful, healthy boy."

My eyes scan hers, waiting for her to say more. She said boy—singular.

"And the others?"

She shakes her head as a tear rolls down her cheek. "I'm so sorry. We lost them."

We.

There is no we.

She didn't have triplets. I did.

I failed.

I didn't provide a good enough home for them. I didn't

eat healthily enough. Exercise enough. Take my vitamins. Reduce my anxiety. I didn't do enough.

I failed.

And now they are gone.

I want to scream, break things, explode into a million pieces.

My grief doesn't allow it. My grief streams down my face in burning silent tears. Tears that pour down each cheek for each of the children I've lost.

My tears are the only external sign of my pain. Everything else I keep inside. The pain rages through my veins like branding fire until my heart can't pump the agony through any longer. It flees from my body to go with my children. I no longer have a heart. A soul. A purpose.

I'm nothing.

I know the woman is hugging me, trying to comfort me, but I don't feel her arms. I'm numb. I feel nothing anymore. I doubt I will ever feel anything ever again.

"The couple is here to adopt the boy," she says. Those words get through the pain.

She waits; I don't say anything.

"There is still time. You can still keep him. You'd make a great mother."

"No, I'd make a terrible mother." Even if I wouldn't, I won't bring a child into my world. He'd end up dead just like my other two children.

"Do you want to hold him before…?" she trails off.

I shake my head.

"Dear, I really think you'll regret not meeting him before you give him up."

My tears stop, and I push back out of her arms as the pain settles into my body. I might as well get used to it. This is my life now—an all-consuming amount of loss. Everywhere I go, I'll feel it. Nothing will take the pain away. Nothing.

"No! I don't want to hold him. I killed them! It's my fault they are dead. If I hold him, I'll just end up killing him too!"

I notice someone at the door, but then he's gone as soon as I get a glance. A lock of blonde hair is all I see as he walks away from me.

Good riddance.

He's the only one who could ease my pain right now. The only boy who would know the exact words to say. The only boy who could love me. And he can't do that—loving me is dangerous.

Plus, I want to feel all the pain. I don't want him to take it away. Not now, not ever.

That whole story was a lie.

The nurse lied to me!

All three of my children survived, not just one. They are all alive. I didn't fail. Langston overhearing that my children died was a lie. All of it.

The pain I've carried with me since that day was a lie.

I have three kids.

None of them are mine.

I didn't fail them that day, but I have now.

Atlas was taken by Maxwell.

Rose was taken by Phoenix.

Declan was taken by Corbin.

Three kids—all taken.

All because I didn't do something sooner. After seeing Atlas myself, I was sure that Corbin and Waylon claiming they had my child was a lie. They had to be bluffing. I knew the second I saw Atlas that he was mine.

Even though I saw the similarities between Rose and me when I saw her, I convinced myself that she was Langston's.

If I hadn't been so afraid, then maybe I could have prevented this. I could have done more to stop it.

I stare at Langston, who is still processing everything. He's basically been frozen in place, his eyes wide, his lips parted, his hair wild since he found out the truth. Rose isn't his child. I have three kids all gone.

I can't imagine how he's processing this.

For a moment, I thought he could have been the one telling me my children died the day they were born. I thought he hated me that much and wanted to punish me.

But despite all the lies we've told each other over the years, he wouldn't tell me that. When he realized Rose wasn't biologically his—it shocked him, hurt him. There is no hiding or faking the kind of pain that comes with losing a child.

If it wasn't Langston who was behind pretending my children died and hiding them from me, then who was it?

It seems important to find out.

But right now, I have more important things to worry about. I need to ensure Langston hasn't gone into shock and figure out a way to protect all three of my kids that are with three separate monsters. I have no idea if Langston is still willing to do this with me or not. Now that he realizes he actually has no biological children, he could just run—file for divorce and live his life. He has no loyalty to me.

In some ways, it might be better if he did. The longer he stays with me, the higher the possibility of him falling in love with me. Other than getting my children back, the next most important thing to me is ensuring he doesn't fall for me.

But what if he already has?

"Langston?" I speak tentatively.

He runs his hand through his hair and immediately snaps back out of his trance.

"Talk to me. What's going through your head?" I ask.

My heart skips waiting for his answer. Somehow this is more important than all the other words he's given me.

"We have three kids we have to get back."

There's that word again—*we*. We have three kids. He speaks about them as if they are his. I guess even though they are all biologically mine, he has a much closer relationship with at least two of them. They call him father. It's clear in his eyes and the words he uses that he won't let that change any time soon.

He grabs my neck and yanks me into his chest until I'm consumed with his smell—pine, sweat, sex—that's him. For a second, I can breathe again. *Would this have happened if, instead of walking away from my hospital room, he walked toward me? Would I have felt like I could breathe again? Like I could face another second of a day? Would I have kept enough of my heart to keep living instead of turning in a shell?*

"I hate you," he says.

I love you.

Fuck. Fuck!

He's not supposed to love me, and I'm not supposed to love him. I don't have a heart left to love him with, *right?*

Something is keeping him from saying the actual words, though, so instead of saying he loves me, he says he hates me. *Maybe he senses the fear in me? Maybe he thinks I'd run if he said he loves me? Maybe he's too stubborn to say the actual words?*

Whatever it is that is preventing him from saying the words I'll hold on to that for as long as I can. It doesn't actually change anything, but it makes me feel like we are safe for a few more minutes.

"I hate you more," I say back.

He smiles, knowing the truth of my words. That's what we do—we lie.

"What are we going to do?" I ask.

"We are going to get our kids back. We are going to get the damn treasure. And we are going to kill anyone who gets in our way."

He speaks his words as if it's already happened, without fear. He's not afraid of failing because it's not a possibility. We are going to get our kids back.

I, on the other hand, am not so sure.

"Hey," he lifts my chin as if sensing that I need comforting. "I'm not going to let anything happen to those kids—all three of them. I love them. They are mine as much as they are yours. I won't let anyone hurt them. We are going to get them back and then never let them out of sight again. Beckett won't be babysitting again; no one will. We'll homeschool them, do whatever it takes to keep them safe. I'm telling you the truth, huntress. Believe every word I'm telling you."

His lips lower, and he seals his promise to me with a kiss. Our lips touch only for a second, but with that kiss, he breathes new life into me.

"What do we do now?" I ask, my head spinning, trying to decide between getting the treasure to pay the ransom to get our kids back and going after them now before getting the treasure.

"Now, we get the crew together. We fight. We get the treasure, and we get our kids."

The crew—he means Enzo, Kai, Zeke, Siren, Beckett.

"Do you trust them after what they did?"

He nods. "I think we've punished them enough. We have three kids to keep safe, being kept in three separate locations. We need their help."

I don't want to trust anyone, not even them. Beckett

failed to keep my kids safe. The others betrayed us and manipulated us to try and get us to like each other. But we need help, and they are the closest thing to family that we have.

Langston calls for a car, and then we are headed back to the airport. We are in our private plane in record time. I should ask Langston about the treasure, about what he found out about what we have to do next. But all I can think about is my kids and about what Langston said about Atlas being sick.

I have to choose my words carefully, so he doesn't know that I was lying. I had no idea that Atlas was sick and dying. If I did, of course, I would have done what I could to help him. Langston holding on to that little piece of hate might be the only thing that ends up saving him in the end, but I have to know what happened.

I'm lying against Langston's chest as the plane takeoffs. "Tell me about when Atlas was sick. How did you save him?"

2

LANGSTON

I DON'T WANT to talk to her about Atlas being sick. Up until this point, it was the worst time of my life. I had her child, and he was dying. Terminal, the doctors said. I had to live with the fact that Liesel knew and did nothing.

But did she really know? The fear she feels about him now is real. I can't imagine she wouldn't have felt the same fear then if she had known. She would have tried to save him, just like I did.

Liesel lies to protect those she cares about. *So why is she lying to me?*

Right now isn't the time to get the truth from her.

I can't talk in great detail about Atlas. It will break me. Although, she deserves to hear a sliver of the truth even if she won't give it to me, so I say a single sentence and hope she reads into it.

"I went to the end of the world to find a cure for him."

She sits up, her eyes blinking as she soaks in my words, trying to decipher what I'm not saying. Her eyes light up, and her head tilts. She's smart—it took her less than three seconds to realize what I'm not saying.

"The cure that Siren and Zeke had. That's why you went after it? For Atlas?"

I nod.

I would have done anything for that boy. I'll continue to do anything for him.

"Thank you for everything, killer."

There is so much truth behind her words. But I didn't do it for her—I did it for him.

She takes my hand in hers, and then we think about the kids the rest of the flight. About Atlas and Rose, who were taken from us. About Declan, who neither of us has met. And about how together we will do whatever it takes to save them.

I glance at her stomach, and something stirs inside me. I have five lives to worry about—Atlas, Rose, Declan, Liesel, and the baby in her womb.

———

Liesel and I drop hands as we walk up the porch to Kai and Enzo's house. Sure, we are together. We're married. We are in this fight together. But we don't want anyone in the house to look at us as a couple. We don't want them to think they somehow were in the right to kidnap us and try to form a bond between us. Our bond has nothing to do with them. It has everything to do with us.

Liesel and I have always been a couple, even when we fought it, even when we hated each other, even when we were apart, even when we lost. It's always been us—even when being together means a lifetime of pain. There is no stopping us.

We give each other a knowing look before I open the door without knocking and step into the three-story mansion. We don't have to be holding each other's hand to gain strength from each other. We don't even have to be sharing the same oxygen. The strength we possess is from knowing that no matter how much we fuck up, lie, cheat, or kill, we are unstoppable together.

We don't even have to say we love each other for it to be true. We just always have.

Kai comes fluttering into the hallway. I'm sure her security system notified her of our arrival.

"Living room, now," I say, marching past her with Liesel right behind me.

Kai nods. She's not used to taking orders from other people, but if she wants to help, Liesel and I will be the ones in charge, not her.

We walk into the living room, where I find Enzo, Zeke, and Siren already on the couches. Siren's eyes are puffy, like she's been crying. Zeke rubs her back in slow circles, like that is somehow going to bring my kids back. Enzo sits sternly, completely lost in thought.

Then I spot Beckett walking in from the kitchen. He looks like a wreck. Puffy eyes, pale skin, a slumped curve of his spine as he walks. The pain he feels is immense—good. He had the most important job. I trusted him. He failed.

He doesn't apologize. He knows there is no use. There is nothing he can say that will bring my kids back.

Liesel walks over to him. I expect her to yell at him for failing. He deserves it. He deserves to be punched in the face and kicked in the balls. The suffering he's feeling is nothing compared to what Liesel and I are going through.

Liesel wraps her arms around him. "We'll get them back. It's not your fault. We should have known not to trust Phoenix or Maxwell. We'll get them back."

He rubs her back with his arm. "No, don't blame yourself. Blame me."

"We do," I say, answering for her.

She shoots me an angry glare.

"It's okay. I can take it. Hate me, not yourself," Beckett says.

She shakes her head and then pulls him into the living room. She chooses to sit next to him on the loveseat. Kai sits next to Enzo. I stay standing, looking down at them all.

"Tell me we already know where they took them. Tell me we already know where they are hidden. Tell me we already have eyes on them." I look between everyone sitting in this room moping, crying, and emotional. The only people who have the right to feel that way are Liesel and me; everyone else has a job to do.

"St. Kitts," Siren and Zeke say.

"Cancun," Kai and Enzo say.

"Atlanta," Beckett says.

I let out a breath. Thank god for them. They may have pissed me off and betrayed us before, but damn do they know how to do their jobs when we need them to.

I look to Liesel, who looks to be near tears at their answers. The question is, *who do we go with?* There are only two of us, and we have three kids to save. *How do we choose?*

"Good. Get a team and plan together to go with you. I want each of you to have a detailed plan in half an hour, then we move."

I storm out onto the back deck, suddenly needing air to breathe as I realize I'm one person, and I can't go after three kids myself at the same time. I'm not superman. I have to trust that others can do their jobs.

I hear the sliding door open and then close, and I know Liesel is standing out on the deck with me.

"How do we decide?" I ask her.

She steps next to me and then grips the railing like her life depends on it. She doesn't answer right away. *How could she? How do you choose between children?*

"We don't," she finally says.

"What?"

"We let our friends go. We let them do their best. And then we go help the one who fails."

The ocean crashes hard against the shoreline at her words. We both stare out at the sea, knowing that's the best plan. But it feels impossible to stay put when my kids are in danger.

My kids.

They will always be my kids. I don't care whose blood runs through their veins—they are mine. Just like the woman to my left, who is wearing my ring. She may have only married me because of a stupid quest, but I'm not giving her up.

I do know something that I can do while we wait to figure out which rescue team is going to need our help the most. I dig into my pocket and pull out the envelope that has the next task in it. I have to complete this task before we can head to Tokyo to get the final task and the location of the treasure. A treasure we can use to get the kids back if all else fails.

I open the envelop and pull out the note. Liesel notices me, but she's content to just stare at the ocean.

I read the note.

Make her fall in love with you so deeply that nothing can pull you apart.

I read the words twice through, trying to ensure that I'm reading them correctly. Make my wife fall in love with me. I'm pretty sure she already is, even though she won't admit it. She won't say the damn words, not that I have either.

How do I prove we love each other so much that nothing will pull us apart? Especially if we won't even say the words?

I've spent my entire life hating her, and she hating me. Hating her is easier, but you can't hate someone without first loving them. The hate was more because we couldn't be together than because we truly hated each other.

This should be an easy task, but it won't be for so many reasons. Liesel is stubborn, and for whatever reason, she's scared to love me and for me to love her. She won't admit to loving me easily. Not only do I have to get her to admit it, but I have to be able to prove it to a stranger when we go to collect the next clue.

I fiddle with the edge of the crisp white paper before it slips through my hands. It dances high in the sky as the wind takes hold of it before dipping into the ocean.

Liesel and I both watch the piece of paper disappear into the water. Liesel could just as easily slip through my fingers.

Getting Liesel to truly love me is going to take everything I have. But that was my plan anyway from the second I said I do. There is no going back, not after she's mine. Fuck the consequences.

No—there are no consequences of her loving me. If Liesel gives me all of her love, I will protect it with everything I have. I will give her the world. I will kill any man or woman who stands against her. Being loved by her would be one of the greatest honors of my life.

I just can't love her in return. Not openly, not in the way she deserves.

The note didn't say that I need to love her, though. It just said that she needs to love me.

I can make her fall in love with me so hard that nothing will break us up. We can be a family once we get the kids back, along with the new edition that I feel in her womb.

"Do you know what you need to do?" Liesel asks, still not looking at me.

"Yes, I can do it easily."

"Good." She nods.

Get her to love me without falling completely in love myself, that shouldn't be too hard.

But I already know this is only half of the task. Last time she had to betray me, and I had to forgive her. So this time, I have to get her to fall for me, *but what will she have to do?*

3

LIESEL

I was dying to know as I watched it flutter into the ocean. Langston won't tell me, though. He can't tell me, just as I couldn't tell him that my mission was to betray him.

What pain is Langston going to have to inflict on me?

It won't be anything compared to the agony I'm feeling knowing all three of my children's lives are in danger.

Outside, rain starts as I stand in the living room hopelessly staring out a window, waiting for news. News that the teams have arrived at the locations, news that they've succeeded in getting through, news that my kids are safe.

I hate standing in Enzo and Kai's house doing nothing, but I know we need to wait. We need to be ready to go if one of them fails.

I hear Langston walking up behind me, but I don't turn around to face him. All I want is news that my kids are safe. Or news of which direction we should head—anything but doing nothing.

I count the raindrops as they run down the window. I

grip the neck of my oversized white T-shirt, just needing something to grip onto.

I feel Langston's hand on my wrist, and he gently gets me to let go of my shirt before he laces his fingers with mine.

I go to pull away, not wanting to be with anyone right now, but he tugs me back. I finally glance at him. His pupils are dilated, his cheeks flushed, the vein in his neck is bulging, and his breathing is erratic.

"I'm just as scared to lose them as you are. We are in this together," he tugs me to him as his other hand strokes my back.

"I don't want to be comforted right now. I want to feel all the stress and anxiety. I failed them. I deserve to feel this way."

He shakes his head, obviously disagreeing, but he doesn't say anything. He doesn't let me go either.

"Let's eat."

I look at him like he's crazy. There is no way I can eat at a time like this.

"We need to have our strength if we have to go help. We are eating," he commands.

"No." There is no possible way I could eat right now.

He frowns. "Huntress, do you want to get your kids back?"

"Of course."

"Then eat."

"No, I'll just throw it up. I'm too nervous."

He narrows his eyes at me suspiciously, like he thinks I'm lying.

Finally, I yank my hand free of his grasp.

"Huntress," he says my name like he's begging me. "Trust me, if you want to do something to help the kids, then you need to spend time with me. Preferably eating, but we can also come up with something else to do if you don't want to eat."

I study him, trying to determine what he's not saying. My eyebrows jump up as I realize what he's not saying—this has to do with the note.

The note is the key to getting the treasure, which might be the only way we can get the kids back if our teams fail. *But what did the note say? What does he have to do?*

"Trust me, huntress. I won't hurt you," Langston says, brushing my hair off my shoulder as he leans in and tenderly kisses my neck. Shivers tingle down my body at the soft touch. It feels wrong to feel anything remotely near pleasant when my kids are in danger.

"It's not wrong to feel connected to me right now. It's not wrong to feel good when the world has turned bad. Don't ever feel guilty for feeling something for me, no matter what is going on, no matter who is in danger."

"All I feel for you is hate," I say softly as my thumb plays with the ring on my finger. The ring has started to disintegrate since it's made of stems and thorns.

Langston wraps his arms around me from behind and pulls me into a hug. "Have dinner with me."

I close my eyes as I lean against his hard chest, feeling calmer with his arms around me. I nod against him even though my stomach churns at the thought of food.

Langston leads me out onto the deck, and I gasp at the sight. The small circular table has a white table cloth, a bouquet of fresh flowers, two lit candles, two plates filled with food, and two wine glasses filled with red wine.

"Is someone else here with us? I thought Kai sent all the staff away so we could be alone?"

"She did. I did this; you were in such a trance you didn't notice."

He leads me over to the chair that has a better view of the

ocean, pulls the chair out, and then waits until I sit. He's being such a gentleman. It's strange.

I smile weakly at him as he takes his seat across from me.

He flashes me a much more sincere smile in return. His actually reaches his eyes. It's meant to soothe my nerves, but it just makes me more anxious as I try to guess what it is he's going to have to do to me. *Betray me? Hurt me? Ruin me?*

He's the only man who has the power to do any of those things—the only person in the world outside of my kids who can hurt me.

His smile drops when he reads my mood, or maybe he can actually read my thoughts.

"I'm not going to hurt you," he says.

"You don't always get a say in whom you hurt."

Our eyes lock for a second in the pain that is our world before the smell of the food finally hits my nose, and I glance down at my plate. It makes me laugh.

"I made your favorite foods," he says, his voice full of pride.

I bite my lip to hide a smile. It's boxed macaroni and cheese with cut-up hot dogs. A giggle escapes despite how hard I tried to hide it.

"Don't laugh. Is macaroni and cheese not still your favorite food?" He says it so seriously that I laugh even harder.

"No, nowadays I prefer my pasta with some actual nutrients in it. Nothing with more chemicals in it than actual food."

He laughs finally. "I know, but Kai and Enzo's fridge didn't have much to make anything except what the kids like. So it was this or frozen pizza, and since I've already made you frozen pizza, I thought this would work best."

I shake my head with a smile as I pick up my fork and stab a piece of the macaroni before taking a bite. The smell overwhelms my senses and flips my stomach. I don't want to eat, but I need to try—Langston's right about that. I start chewing, but something is off.

"Um…it's crunchy," I say.

Langston's nose is curled up as he chews his own bite. He spits his food out into his napkin, which gives me permission to do the same without insulting him or insinuating that I'm pregnant or something.

"What did you do to it?" I ask, now inspecting the pasta to see that half of it looks completely undercooked, while the other half looks overcooked.

"I followed the directions on the box." He frowns before testing a bite of the hot dog.

I roll mine around on the plate and sink my fork in it, realizing that it takes too much effort to sink the tongs of the fork into the flesh of the hot dog. I put my fork down and watch Langston try a bite.

His face turns green, and he barely gets his napkin to his mouth before he spits it out.

"So I shouldn't be expecting my new husband to cook for me every night then?" I joke.

He runs his hand through his hair, and I notice some sweat coming through his T-shirt.

"I promise I'm a better cook than this. I've made boxed macaroni and cheese and hot dogs a hundred times for Rose and Atlas. I don't know what happened?" He stares at the food again incredulously, like it did something wrong to him.

His cheeks pink. He's sweating even more now. I don't know why he's so nervous, but I try to ease his mind by lifting my wine glass.

His eyes bulge as he watches me drink the wine. I know he thought for sure I was pregnant, but I'm not. Short of peeing on a stick, drinking my wine will have to convince him.

Except, one taste and I'm spitting the liquid out as I get a mouthful of cork.

"What's wrong?" Langston asks.

"Um…the cork disintegrated into the bottle. It's more cork than wine at this point." I put the glass back on the table.

Langston inspects his glass, takes a small taste, realizes I'm right, and then sets the glass back down in a huff.

"I'm sorry. I can order delivery."

I shake my head. "It's okay. I'm too nervous to eat much anyway. I'll eat once I know the kids are safe."

He nods with a frown. "What happens when this is all over?"

"What do you mean?"

"I mean with us. What kind of life do you want? Where should we live? What do you want out of life?"

I look out at the ocean. The sun has begun to set. We should get some news from how the missions are going. "I can't imagine this ever being over."

"It will be sooner than you think. What do you imagine our lives like then?"

Our.

That word sounds so nice leaving his mouth. We haven't had 'our' since we were kids. I'm not foolish enough to think that just because I have a ring on my finger that anything is going to change. I'll still live alone, and Langston will continue to be an incredible father.

Langston stands up then. It's clear he's not happy with whatever he sees on my face. He takes my hands as he kneels in front of me.

"Stop thinking that your life going forward is going to include anything but me and the kids in it," he says.

I shake my head. "You can't make promises like that, killer. You might hate me when this is over."

"I already hate you," he says with a wry smile.

"For real," I say. When he says he hates me, it means I love you, or as close to love as he can feel. "And nothing will change once the kids are safe. They aren't mine, not really. I'd make a terrible mother."

His eyes narrow as he clenches my hands tighter. "You'd make a wonderful mother."

I want to argue more, but there is no use doing that now, so I don't.

"Once this is all over, I see us building a house on a private island somewhere. We have more money than we need. We'll live on the island, the five of us."

I'd rather live in the house he already built—our dream house. I don't care that he and Phoenix lived in it together already—it's mine.

"We'll live happily ever after as we watch the kids grow up until they leave us to start their own lives. We'll get a dog, maybe some cats to fill the house while we wait for grand-children. Maybe we'll start a charity for underprivileged kids."

He grips my hands tighter until they feel clammy. I don't know what the lead up is. He's about to drop the other shoe, something that will bring my world crashing down like always. I'm not ready for him to hurt me, even if he's doing it to get the treasure and help bring back the kids.

I see him reach for something in his pocket, but he misjudges and bumps the table. The plates rattle around, distracting me from the doom I'm feeling.

I watch as one of the candles twirls around before knocking over onto the table. A second later, flames dance over the tablecloth.

"Langston," I say, entranced by the flame.

"You love it?" he asks. "If not, I can get you a different one."

I have no idea what he's talking about; all I can see is the fire growing bigger behind him. He has no clue. He's focused on whatever annihilation of my heart he's supposed to be doing to me.

"Langston!" I shout, still frozen.

The single word is enough to get Langston's attention this time.

"Shit," he curses as he drags me away from the table before I catch on fire.

He drags me into the house before running back outside.

I don't watch him through the window. I don't care that our makeshift date or whatever it was Langston was trying to accomplish got ruined. I'm relieved that we didn't get to the hurting me part.

I walk into the living room, completely exhausted. I want the phone to ring to tell me that the kids are safe, but I'm more scared I'll get a call to find out one is dead. So I'd rather not hear the phone ringing. I'd rather just stay in this moment of fearful pain.

I lie down on the carpet in the middle of the room. I don't know why I do it. I just need to lie down fully, and I don't have the energy to walk to a bed.

I hear a commotion outside before Langston finally walks into the living room. His shirt is gone. His chest is glistening with sweat and dirt. His hair untamed on top of his head.

"That was a disaster," he says.

"I don't know. It kind of feels like all our dates should be like that. It would be more us."

His lip twitches as he puts one leg on either side of my hips before lowering himself until he's straddling me.

"Which is why I'm not going to try to be romantic, not anymore."

He was trying to be romantic? Why?

He grabs my left hand and pulls out a diamond ring. "This ring is yours forever."

He starts to push the ring onto my finger. He doesn't take the ring made of flowers off; he just pushes the new ring right on top.

"Just as I'm yours forever."

His eyes pour into me, vowing his love. I can't let him make such a promise. I can't let him fall any more than he already has. I can't destroy him any more than I already have. So I look at the ring instead.

My heart clenches when I see it. It's a simple oval diamond on a gold band. Timeless, elegant, and exactly what I said I wanted when I was a kid.

He remembered.

4

LANGSTON

That thought repeats through my head like a raging wildfire. We tried a simultaneous attempt to get them all back, but all of our intel was wrong. I thought for sure we'd get one, possibly even two back tonight. Then Liesel and I could meet up with everyone to go rescue whoever remained.

I never thought I'd have to decide which kid to save first. I hated making the decision, but one look at Liesel told me there was no way she was able to decide. Her body was shaking, and I'd never seen her so white. Even now, as we drive through to the German countryside, her body is still trembling. I grip her hand in the passenger seat next to me.

I chose Rose because she seems to be in the most danger, and we have the best lead to get her back. I have no idea if I chose correctly or not. If I chose wrong, and we lose one of them because of me, then I'll never forgive myself.

I've never been so terrified in my life, but I refuse to let Liesel know that. She's been through enough. My job as her husband is to protect her the best I can. So that's what I'm going to do—protect her and our kids at all costs.

29

I pull into the driveway of the old house that Enzo and Kai are keeping Phoenix. I don't speak to Liesel as I climb out. She manages to get out of the car before I run around to her. I take her hand—the one that now has a real ring on it. A ring I thought could be the key to her starting to admit her true feelings for me. How stupid I was to think that giving her a ring would change anything, especially in a time like this.

I hold her hand all the same, and we race inside. I don't knock; I just open the door, taking no notice of the color of the house, the decorations. Nothing but finding Enzo and Kai. Nothing but finding Phoenix. Nothing but finding my daughter.

She may not be my blood, but she's mine nonetheless.

Enzo and Kai greet us as we rush through the house.

"Phoenix is in the basement. We haven't gotten anything out of her yet, but being tortured by someone you know is always more effective than a stranger," Enzo says.

I nod, agreeing.

My eyes cut to Liesel. She's been through enough. I take both of her hands in mine as I face her. "Talk to Kai, get all the information she has. Drink some tea to settle your stomach, maybe eat something. I'll get the information we need to find Rose."

"I should talk to Phoenix."

I shake my head. "You're the huntress. You will hunt to the ends of the earth to find Rose."

She nods, realizing what I'm saying. The whites of her eyes grow wide around her dark orbs. "You're the killer."

And I'll kill Phoenix or anyone else who threatens my children.

Kai walks over and takes Liesel by her hand, leading her over to a small two-seat dining room table. I know Kai will take care of Liesel while I do what has to be done.

"Take me to the basement," I say to Enzo.

He nods and heads to a door down the hallway. He opens it for me with focused attention. "Do you want me to go down with you?"

"No."

I take the stairs two at a time. We have no time to waste. This woman knows where Rose is. She might know where Atlas and Declan are.

I hit the bottom step and then flick on the lights. Knowing what I'd see didn't stop my heart from skipping a beat. Phoenix is beaten, bloodied, and crumpled on the floor with her wrists tied together. My jaw ticks in anger, and my body shakes.

I was once married to this woman—or fake married, whatever.

I thought she was the mother of my child. She acted like a great mother and stepmother. At least, that's what I thought.

My concern quickly turns to rage at this woman.

She looks up, her eyes squinting because of the abrupt change from dark to light. She may think I'm the light about to come to save her, but she'd be very wrong.

I grab her by the back of her neck, yanking her hair and forcing her onto her feet.

Phoenix stares at her feet rather than look at me.

I tilt my head, trying to force her eyes on me with just my glare.

"Look at me, Phoenix." My voice is low and sure. I won't be leaving this basement without answers. Phoenix is the one who will decide if she lives or leaves this basement in pieces.

She still doesn't lift her head to look at me, so I do it for her.

She groans, but I finally get to look her in the eyes. I want nothing but the truth from her, and the only way I can ensure that is if I look her in the eyes.

"Where is Rose?" I ask calmly. *How am I calm?* I have no idea. I just know I should start calm and collected. Then, if she doesn't answer, I can turn wild.

"Is that the question you want to ask me first?" she has the audacity to say.

"Yes," I growl.

Her eyes lighten, and a sly smile lifts on her cheek. "You're always asking the wrong questions. Always putting faith in the wrong people. I'll answer your question, but it will be the last one I answer."

I frown.

What other questions do I have? A million, but none seem as important.

My eyes roam up and down her broken body. I don't know how many bones Enzo broke; I just know that he did. Bile slips up my throat at everything this woman and I have been through together.

I married her.

Fucked her.

Thought she was the mother of my child.

I gave her my most precious possessions to take care of— my children.

I realize a question I need answering before she tells me where Rose is.

"Did you ever hurt them? Abuse them? Did you get your jollies off on hurting them?"

She looks me dead in the eyes. "I never hurt them."

A sea of relief floods me at her words. But why should I believe her?

"I don't believe you."

She shrugs. "That's up to you, but my conscience is clean."

She's baiting me. *But why?*

"I thought you loved me. I thought that's why you married me. Not to control me and get my children to trust you until the time came for you to take them."

"You're upset that I didn't love you? That our marriage was a scam? Our marriage would have been a scam whether or not I took Rose from you. You never loved me. It was always her."

She's not wrong.

"You lied to me! You tricked me."

"You lied to me. You tricked me," she says right back.

I want to scream. I want to rip her apart and then put her back together only to rip her apart again.

I don't trust her.

I don't know if she ever hurt the kids.

I don't even know if she's hiding Rose somewhere safe.

But I have one more question before I find out where Rose is.

"Why? Why start all of this? Why marry me? Why take the kids? Why is Liesel's treasure so important?"

She licks her lips and tosses her hair out of her face. "Now, you're finally asking the right questions."

5

PHOENIX

"WHAT ARE YOU DOING?" Corbin's voice makes me jump.

I turn, standing on the small step stool in the kitchen. "I'm trying to reach the mixing bowl. I'm making brownies."

He shakes his head like I'm crazy as he rushes over to me, worried my very life hangs in the balance. "Get down, right now."

He holds out his hand and helps me down the two steps. "Keep your feet on the ground. Or preferably, put your feet up."

I roll my eyes. "So, are you going to be cooking me brownies then?"

He climbs up the ladder and grabs the mixing bowl. "Waylon!"

I smile as my other brother runs into the room.

"What?" His hair is frazzled, and his eyes big with concern as he looks to my swollen belly and then up to my face, expecting some kind of emergency. I'm not due for at least another month, but my three brothers all treat me like I'm going to pop at any second.

"Do I need to bring the car around?" Maxwell darts into the kitchen.

I just laugh at the three idiots. I love them, but they are all too much sometimes.

"No! Nothing is wrong. Apparently, Dr. Corbin here has decided that I'm no longer able to climb the two steps up on a step ladder to grab a mixing bowl or cook myself some brownies," I say.

"Brownies, I'm on it!" Waylon says, grabbing the bowl from Corbin before flying over to the pantry to start grabbing ingredients.

I sigh. There is no use arguing with them.

"You. Couch. Now," Corbin says.

Maxwell runs to my side, taking my hand like I can't even walk without support. He helps me into the living room and onto the sofa.

"When is Martin getting off?" I ask Maxwell.

I know that Martin is working on his last deal before the babies arrive. It's a deal with a partner we've worked with a hundred times—a Mr. Dunn. Smuggling drugs is a dangerous business, but it's made my family infinite amounts of money. The business has made us all happy.

Until I fell in love.

Until I got pregnant.

Now, my fiancé and three brothers will stop at nothing to protect me and the babies I carry—including them giving up the business that has provided for us all these years.

What are we going to do once we give up smuggling drugs?

Be incredibly fucking happy; that's what.

We have more money than we need to survive.

We have three babies on the way that we can all give plenty of love to.

We all have hobbies we can spend more time enjoying.

My brothers can find time to date—to fall in love and fill this house with more babies, more happiness.

Just one more job, and then this is all over.

My eyes drift shut. It's exhausting work carrying around triplets.

I inhale sweet chocolatey goodness.

My eyes open just as Waylon brings me a plate filled with brownies.

I smile as he sets the plate on my stomach.

"Thank you," I say.

He glances at his watch. "Corbin and I have to go meet Martin to execute our sale with Dunn. You'll be okay with Maxwell watching you?"

I nod, my smile brightening. The sooner they leave, the sooner they finish the job, and we can get on to the next chapter of our lives. Selling drugs is a dangerous business, but my brothers and Martin are very good at it. I have no worries they'll make it back just fine.

"Yep, thanks to you, I don't have to eat any of his terrible cooking."

He grins and then leans down and kisses me on the forehead. "I love keeping my nieces and nephews fed." He leans down close to my belly. "Stay in there until we get back."

I just roll my eyes and watch as Waylon heads out, followed by Corbin, who just nods in my direction before taking off.

Maxwell collapses on the couch next to me. "So what are we watching while we stuff our faces?"

———

Maxwell's phone buzzes as we watch another house-hunting show.

I pop another piece of brownie into my mouth while

Maxwell answers, assuming it's Corbin or Waylon calling to say the job is done and they are headed back.

Maxwell's smile immediately drops as he listens.

"What is it?" I ask.

He stands, not answering me as he whispers something into the phone.

My heart stops, which isn't good since it's supplying blood to not only me but the three babies growing inside of me.

I scramble to my feet, which is easier said than done.

I walk quickly through the house, each step forcing blood through my already breaking heart. I can feel the change, the shift. I know without any words that Martin is gone. I don't feel him anymore. I feel nothing but numbness.

No, that's crazy to think. He's not dead, just injured. He can't be dead.

I spot Maxwell out on the back deck, pacing, still on the phone. He's trying to protect me, but I have to know.

I waddle outside, moving as fast as my swollen feet will take me. I throw the door open and step out into the chilly air.

Maxwell drops the phone when he sees me.

"What happened?" I ask, using all my oxygen to get the words out.

He shakes his head. "You should be inside, sitting down." He rubs his neck. "No, maybe we should head to the hospital."

Head to the hospital?

"What happened to Martin? How bad is it?"

He closes the distance between us and takes my hands in his. "We all love you. We are all here for you. Whatever happens next, you will always have the three of us to love and protect you."

The three of us.

"What. Happened?"

He opens his mouth with tears in his eyes. "Dunn betrayed us. He took the drugs without paying. He attacked us." His throat catches, his tears fall, and the pain ricochets off him and onto me. "Martin—he didn't make it."

I feel myself falling, collapsing in his arms as my heart stops. My heart belonged to Martin. He was my everything. If he's gone, I don't want to live. I want to be gone too.

My body decides for me as I faint, my eyes roll back in my head, and I'm gone.

6

LIESEL

I SNUCK HALFWAY downstairs during the middle of Phoenix's story, but I heard enough for my heart to break. I heard enough to understand her pain. Enough that I can understand why she wants revenge, why the whole family does.

My father took the most important person from her.

He took the love of her life.

And the trauma of losing him caused her to lose the babies. She didn't explicitly say she lost her babies, but I can feel it in her tears. She lost everything, and her brothers, loyal to her above everything, shared her pain.

They want to make me pay for what my father did to them. That's why they took my kids, that's why they want the treasure as payback for what was stolen from them all those years ago.

I can't blame them for feeling this way. I'm sure I would react much the same if they had taken Langston or my kids from me.

When Phoenix finishes speaking, she collapses in Langston's arms. Just like she did in the story—like the

41

trauma of retelling her experience brought her right back to those feelings.

I peer down to watch Langston hold a limp Phoenix in his arms. He hasn't spoken since she started telling her story, so I have no idea what's going on in his head. I'm also not sure if he knows I'm here or not. If he does, he hasn't said anything.

I watch him hold her in his arms, waiting patiently for her to come to. He checks her pulse with his fingers, but I can see from here that she's breathing. Then, he pulls a knife from his pocket and slices through the ropes binding her hands.

"I can't kill her," he says.

He knows I'm here.

"No, you can't," I agree.

"What are we going to do with her?"

"We are going to keep her here until we find Rose."

"And then?"

I have no idea.

Phoenix stirs, her eyes opening in Langston's arms. She takes her time sitting back up, but her eyes find mine. She's wearing black like always. I realize it's because she always in mourning. Every day she feels that loss because of my father.

As much as she hates my family and me, I don't think she would inflict the same pain on me. I don't think she'd hurt or kill any of my kids. She just wants me to suffer a small fraction of the pain she once felt.

That gives me hope that Rose is alive and untouched. It gives me hope that Maxwell and Corbin won't hurt my children either. Corbin may be the oldest and in charge, but Phoenix is the one they follow. She's the one who matters.

I walk down the rest of the stairs and over to where she is still in Langston's arms.

"Where is Rose?" I ask gently.

"My family owns three clubs; each of them is hiding one of your kids. The only way to get in is to play a game. Win the game to get into X, and you'll get Rose back. Pay with your sins and your treasure. Pay with everything you have."

"And if we lose?"

"Then I keep her forever."

LANGSTON

OUR KIDS ARE BEING HELD at three different clubs.

Jesus.

I remember the last "club"—the fucked up yacht masquerade weekend. I don't want to go through that again to get our kids back, let alone three more times. But I'll do anything to get them back, including playing some twisted game meant to torture us.

I feel for Phoenix, maybe because she pretended to be my wife. Maybe because I watched her with Rose and Atlas, and she was a good mother to them. You can't fake that. She cared about them, even if she only did it to hurt Liesel and me.

Maybe it was the story she told, the pain she felt, that has me feeling weak. But whatever the reason, I carry Phoenix upstairs to one of the bedrooms. She fell asleep in my arms, exhausted from telling me her story and from the injuries Enzo inflicted before we got here.

I lay her down on a white comforter with pink flowers on it. I grab a throw blanket draped over a chair in the corner and cover her before I close the door quietly behind me and head back downstairs.

All eyes are on me when I enter the small kitchen.

"Bring Phoenix some food and keep her comfortable," I say.

Enzo's eyebrows shoot up. "Why?"

"She's not a monster. She's just in pain," Liesel answers, giving me the smallest of smiles, letting me know she approves of my actions.

"Did you find out where Rose is?" Kai asks.

"The Brown family owns three clubs. The one on the yacht that we all went to and two others. The children are split between the clubs. We have to win the game at each club in order to get the kid being held there back."

"Well, they owe us one kid already then, since you won before," Enzo says with a growl.

"I need to call Siren," I say.

"I'll call Beckett," Liesel says.

I nod.

Neither of us thinks that any of them would hurt the children, not after Phoenix's story. It doesn't mean we are willing to stop searching and trying to get the kids back as quickly as possible.

I dial Siren's number.

"Hello," Siren answers out of breath.

"Phoenix told me where the kids are and how to get them back."

"Thank god," Siren exhales sharply. We've always been close; she's as torn up as I am about the kids being taken.

"The Browns own three clubs. One is here in Germany. The second is the yacht we were all on."

"Maxwell boarded the yacht this afternoon. We've been chasing him this whole time."

"Then, the third must be where Corbin is holding Declan.

We are going to the club here to get Rose back tonight, and then we can come to the yacht."

"Why these games?"

"Liesel's father caused the deaths of Phoenix's fiancé and unborn babies. This is payback to make us suffer as much as possible. I don't think they will hurt them, though, thank god. But we need to get them back as quickly as possible, obviously."

There's a pause.

"We'll win the yacht game while you get into the club there," she says.

"Siren, you played the game last time. You know what it involves. There is no chance you'll win."

"I owe you. And those kids—" her voice cracks, and I can hear the pain in it.

"Siren?"

"Zeke and I will get Atlas back while you and Liesel get Rose. Has Beckett found Declan yet?"

"No, but Liesel is talking to Beckett now and letting him know to search for a club. That should help them narrow down their search."

"Good."

"Siren, are you sure? Liesel and I can come after we finish here."

"I'm sure. My heart isn't whole until yours is. I don't care who I have to fuck or my husband fucks or kills—we are going to get Atlas back tonight."

"Thank you," I exhale, able to breathe a little easier now that there's hope that two of our kids are going to be safe tonight.

I end the call at the same time Liesel does. Her face is so drained, her eyes heavy, her body frail. She needs sleep, rest, food, but all of that will have to wait until we get the kids back.

"Siren and Zeke are going to enter the yacht club by winning the sex game. They are going to get Atlas back tonight while we get Rose."

Liesel nods her head, tears watering her eyes with a tiny glint of relief.

I pull her into my chest, wishing I could do more to comfort her.

"Beckett said he would find the club. He said if he finds it, he'll enter it too. He'll do whatever it takes to get Declan back."

With Liesel in my arms, it's almost like I can breathe again. Almost.

"We are going to get them back," I say. I'm not sure why I ever doubted my friends. They are all going beyond what I would ever ask them to do to save my children. I automatically forgive them for anything they've done.

"We are going to get them back so they can be with their father," Liesel mumbles into my chest.

I grab her cheeks and force her to look up at me. "We are going to get them back so they can be with their father and mother."

A tear rolls down Liesel's cheek. There is so much pain in that single tear, so much heartbreak.

Heartbreak I won't let her go through alone.

Liesel doesn't think she's deserving of being a mother. She doesn't think she belongs in our kids' lives. She's wrong, and this time I'm not giving her a choice. When we get our children back, she's going to meet them. Then she'll realize just how much they need her in their lives.

8

LIESEL

BECKETT FOUND THE THIRD CLUB, so we're all going to try to rescue them at the same time. We have some really good friends willing to go this far to get our kids back.

I paint my lips with red lipstick as I finish getting ready in the bathroom. My dress is silver and sparkly as it clings to my curves and down to the floor, revealing plenty of cleavage as well. We don't know exactly what we are facing, but we have an idea after the yacht game we played.

It will be difficult and test our limits. Luckily we have none when it comes to getting the kids back.

I don't know if Beckett, Siren, or Zeke will succeed, but I'm beyond grateful that they are willing to try.

There's a light knock on the bathroom door. My stomach rumbles as I stand and open the door.

"You look beautiful," Kai says, standing in the bathroom door.

I smile at her, but it's fake.

"Do you need anything else? Food?"

I shake my head. I can't eat right now, but I don't want to

draw attention to it. Langston will drive me crazy worrying about me.

"I wish there was more Enzo and I could do. Are you sure you don't want us to go with you?"

"You're doing enough staying here and watching Phoenix. Really, you have no idea how much your help means to me."

Kai hugs me. "We are going to get them back. And when we do, we aren't ever going to let them go again."

"I know."

Pain radiates through my body, but I don't let Kai know.

She steps back and holds out a silver mask. I take it from her, a familiar pang shooting through me from the last time I wore a mask like this.

We hear footsteps, and Kai steps back to allow Langston through.

"I'll just be downstairs if you need me," Kai says before leaving.

Then it's just Langston and me.

"Wow," he says as his eyes roam up and down my body. He takes in every curve, every inch of exposed skin, every contour of my face.

For a moment, all I feel is the heat of his eyes gracing my skin. I forget about how scared I am and how my stomach roars with pain and anxiety. For a moment, I feel wanted, desired, lured.

Langston must feel the change, too. Wordlessly, he takes two steps toward me, grabs my neck, and crushes his lips over mine. The kiss is needy and desperate. His tongue pushes into my mouth without asking for permission, without giving me time to think that I shouldn't be feeling any sort of pleasure when my kids' lives are at risk.

The kiss continues despite the tiny whispers of reason

floating in my head, telling me I shouldn't enjoy this. All I deserve to feel is pain.

Langston's tongue disagrees with the thoughts in my head. He pushes them out with each stroke of his tongue until the thoughts flutter away. Finally, when the thoughts have vanished, does he stop the kiss.

"That's why you will make a great mother," he says.

"What?"

"Because you won't even let yourself enjoy a kiss. Your entire thoughts are on the kids. You love them without having met them. That's why you are going to make a great mom."

I take a deep breath. Now isn't the time to argue with him.

My eyes take him in for the first time. He's wearing a tux that I know he rented, yet somehow fits him like a glove. I can see his hardened muscles beneath the black fabric of his jacket and pants. His erection pushes against the zipper. My eyes shoot back up to his face, so he doesn't get the wrong idea and think I want to fuck him. But that's a mistake, too. His hair is tousled, and his face is clean-shaven, making me drool over the sharpness of his jaw. I know I can't go near his eyes. His eyes are a danger zone I'll get lost in.

He pushes his hands into my hair, not caring that he's messing up the curls I spent hours perfecting. He kisses me again—slower, gentler, reminding me that I'm his.

"Whatever it takes," he says, pulling my lips into his mouth once more.

"Whatever it takes," I say, agreeing to his promise.

Then, he locks his fingers with mine and leads me out of the house to the waiting car. We climb in the back, and one of Kai's employees climbs into the front. Langston holds my hand the entire thirty-minute drive to the club, but that doesn't ease the butterflies in my stomach.

The car eases to a stop.

"Look at me," Langston says.

I turn and look at him. He holds up my mask and fastens it around my face. "You're the fiercest, most beautiful, badass woman in there. Nothing will stop you."

"And you're the strongest, most handsome, cruel man in there. Nothing will stop you."

His eyes darken. "I hate you." There is a bite in his words that is meant to stir a reaction.

"I hate you, too." Every time I say the words, or he does, I no longer know the true meaning. I no longer know what the words mean when either of us speaks them, just that they mean a lot.

The car door opens. I step out, taking Langston's hand as he guides me down a sidewalk and inside the club.

We enter the building with blacked-out windows and no sign. There is nothing to indicate what takes place inside.

"Hello, welcome to X. Can I have your name and invite, please?" a gentleman in a tux asks with an iPad in his hands.

"Mr. Langston Pearce and Mrs. Liesel Pearce. Phoenix Brown is who invited us," I say.

Langston practically growls when I spit out his name as my last, making my insides tingle with what it does to him when I claim him as my husband.

"Welcome, Mr. and Mrs. Pearce. The games start in thirty minutes. I'll show you to the bar where you can have a drink while you wait."

He leads us down the hallway and stops at an open door. "Enjoy yourselves."

We walk hand in hand into the room. It's a spacious room, filled with guests in their most formal attire, all sipping various drinks as a woman sings at a piano in the center of the room. The bar is on the far side. All eyes turn to us as we enter. I suspect everyone does this with each new guest, trying to judge the new competition.

I roll my shoulders back, standing taller. Langston stares them all down. We make it clear we are here to win—anything less will not happen.

Together we walk over to a small circular booth in the corner of the room with a good view.

A waitress immediately comes over. "What can I get you to drink?"

"Two of your finest scotches," Langston answers.

I don't know if my stomach can handle a drop of alcohol, but I don't argue. I don't want to appear weak, and I don't want Langston to think something stupid like I'm pregnant or something.

"So what do you think this game is going to involve?" I ask.

"Fucking, pain, torture—the usual."

I nod.

"We are going to get her back. And if we lose, we'll try again and again until we win, or we'll find another way. I'm pretty proficient with a gun, you know."

His comment is meant to make me smile, but I find I can't.

The waitress returns with our drinks, and without thinking, I take a long sip, regretting it immediately as it burns all the way down to my anxious gut.

Langston stares at me curiously but doesn't say anything.

I set my drink down carefully and hold it in my hands while I peruse the faces in the room, trying to determine our biggest competition.

"No one is competition. No one is fighting to get their child back. We'll win," Langston says.

His words are meant to be encouraging, to douse some of

my anxiety, but nothing but seeing Rose, Atlas, and Declan safely in Langston's arms will put out my fear.

We sit quietly until the man with the iPad re-enters the room. "The game is about to begin if you will all follow me."

People toss back the rest of their drinks before standing to follow him out. When I stand, I find my legs trembling. Langston notices, takes my arm, and leads me out. With his hand touching me, I'm calm enough to walk.

We are led into a smaller room containing four round tables, each with five seats. It's then that I realize there are twenty of us here, and I'm the only woman.

Chills race up and down my spine. Something isn't right. There is something that Phoenix didn't tell us, but I'm clueless. It feels like we've just walked into a trap.

Langston notices and stands a little in front of me, letting anyone in the room know they will have to go through him before they get to me. He'd take a bullet for me, not that I'd let him.

The host walks to the front of the room and begins explaining the rules.

"Welcome, gentlemen and Mrs. Pearce. Thank you all for coming. You all know what is at stake. Now for the rules of the game. They are quite simple. You will all be randomly seated at a table, and cards will be distributed to you, each containing a different...dares, shall we call them? Every dare has a point value, based on the card. Each round you will bet which dare, or combination of dares, you are willing to do. The highest bets stay in the game. The lowest bet must do their wagered dare, or dares, to stay in the game.

"Each round, you will have an opportunity to trade in your cards to be dealt new ones. You can trade in all or none of your cards, and you'll be dealt any additional cards to ensure you always have five cards in your hand. Once a winner has been declared at each table, the final round, or rounds, will decide our winner from the group of table winners. There will be a dealer at each table if you have any questions."

There are some murmurs, snide remarks, and grins from the men in the crowd. All of them stare at me like I'm a piece of meat to devour.

"I won't let anyone hurt you," Langston whispers.

"The only way to ensure that is if I quit right now."

"You should; I've got this."

"No, I'll play. We both stay, we double our chances."

"But—"

"I'm staying."

Names are called out as men are assigned different tables.

Then my name is announced; I'm at table two. I just have to figure out how to walk over there without Langston to lean on.

My legs shake as I attempt to strut with everyone's eyes on me, looking at me like I don't belong. I regret the stilettos with every step. One wrong step, and I'm going to fall and lose the game before it even starts.

Somehow I make it to my chair. I feel Langston from across the room. Unlike the last game we played, he's going to be more protective of me. He's going to have limits of what he can watch me endure. I just hope we get to Rose before that happens.

More names are called, and the rest of the men take their seats. Langston ends up at the table nearest to mine. It's nice to feel like he's a partner in the game this time, but I don't know how much good it's going to do.

Four men are eventually sitting at the table with me. All of their eyes are locked on me. I'm the outcast, and they are happy to destroy me. I really wish I knew why I was the only woman here.

I study my opponents as the dealers begin making their

way to the tables. To my immediate left is a middle-aged man that must be a cowboy in a former life. He's decked out in boots, a cowboy hat, and handlebar mustache.

Next is a dark-haired man with slicked-back hair, a too-tight suit, and brown eyes. He's around my age and is wearing a wedding ring.

The third man is wearing a tux, but it does little to cover his rough exterior. Tattoos peek out around his wrists and neck. He has a nasty scar under his right eye that didn't heal properly.

My fourth table-mate is an older gentleman. What's left of his hair is graying around the bald spot on his head. He wears an expensive, ill-fitting tux that screams wealth.

"Good evening, gentleman and ma'am. I'll be your dealer for tonight. If anyone has any questions about how the game is played, then please let me know. Otherwise, let's begin," he says, shuffling what looks like an ordinary deck of cards. He looks around at the five of us, waiting to see if anyone speaks up. When no one does, he begins to deal us each five cards.

A couple of the men pick up the cards as they are dealt one by one and begin studying them. Me and the older man to my right wait until all the cards are dealt before picking up our hand.

"Point values are one for an ace all the way up to thirteen for a king. You can bet up to the full value in your hand or as little as one card. Remember, if you're the lowest bet, you have to do whatever you bet, so don't bet something you aren't willing to do. The deck is a standard 52 card deck, just with dares written on them. Take a moment to study your cards and decide your bet."

I look at my cards. I have two aces, a three, a seven, and a ten.

The aces are easy tasks. The three isn't bad. The seven

starts to hurt. The ten I don't even want to think about. I don't want to know what's on a king.

"Mr. Wilson, you may start the bidding. The bidding will continue around until no one wants to bid any higher," our dealer says.

"Five," the cowboy, Mr. Wilson says.

"Seven," I say.

"Ten," the slick suit says.

"Ten," the tattooed man says.

"Thirteen," the older gentleman says.

"Eighteen," the cowboy says.

Shit.

"Twelve," I say, hoping that I won't have to play my ten and that someone else bids lower.

"Twenty-four," the slick suit says.

"Thirty," the tattooed man says.

"Twenty-five," the older gentleman says.

All eyes fall to me.

Shit.

"Mrs. Pearce, would you like to bid higher? If not, bidding is closed and you lose this round," the dealer says.

There is no point bidding higher. Even if I played all of my cards, it would still only be twenty-two, two lower than the next lowest bid.

I shake my head.

"If everyone would please lay down the cards they bid face down so I can check your bids," the dealer says.

Everyone places their bid cards face down, and he collects them one by one, ensuring the bet that was placed was in fact in their hands.

When the dealer collects my cards, he takes his time reading each of the tasks. He whispers into a microphone and then looks back at the table.

"To continue playing Mrs. Pearce, you owe a drop of

blood, a kiss from a stranger, the removal of one item of clothing, and one lash of a whip. Are you willing to pay your debts?"

"Yes," I say, confidently. I didn't bet anything that I wouldn't be willing to do to get my child back. I would have bet everything I had every time if I had good enough cards.

He nods.

A woman in a slinky black dress walks over, carrying a tray of items stands behind the dealer. "The winner of the round gets to decide if he wants to inflict the debt." He motions behind him. "Or if Miss Kiff here will be inflicting the debt. Mr. Mullock, which will it be?" the dealer asks the tattooed man.

"I would love the pleasure," he says.

"Mr. Mullock and Mrs. Pearce, if you would follow Miss Kiff please," the dealer says.

I stand shakily on my feet. My head spins, and my stomach heaves, wanting to vomit, but not because of this stupid game. The men are going to try and gang up on me, but I have no doubt that I'll win.

We follow Miss Kiff to one side of the room, where I realize there is a small stage. This is part of the game—the show. I'm sure there are plenty of rich people watching our humiliation. There are people standing in line to the stage from each table. Langston isn't among them. I look back and find him sitting at the table, staring at me wide-eyed. The vein on his head is throbbing, and his eyes rage with pain.

Relax, I got this, I mouth to him.

He doesn't relax. If anything, the tension in his body tightens.

I sigh.

I can't worry about him. I need to find a way to win this game without having to endure stupid humiliation.

I don't pay attention to the first man. I hear laughter, then applause as he shrieks in pain. Then it's my turn.

I walk up the three steps onto the rickety stage, pleased with myself for staying upright. I really should have eaten something.

Mr. Mullock steps onto the stage behind me. Miss Kiff and her tray of evil things settles in front of me.

"A drop of blood," she says, handing Mullock the knife.

He takes it from her then encircles me, making a big show of running the blade of the knife over my breasts, then down my stomach.

I can sense Langston in the crowd, ready to jump to my aid at a moment's notice.

"Get on with it," I hiss through my teeth.

He snarls back and then slices the blade superficially across the top of my breast, causing more than a drop of blood to ooze out of my skin. The crowd hisses and snickers.

"So original," I say, not impressed at all by him.

He frowns, putting the knife back on the tray.

"A kiss from a stranger," Miss Kiff says next.

I don't wait for Mullock to take his time deciding how or where he's going to kiss me. I grab his cheeks and plant one on his lips before he even has time to realize what happened.

The crowd chuckles as Mullock growls. "I'm supposed to be inflicting the debt, not you."

I roll my eyes. "Then hurry up; we have a game to play."

"An item of clothing," Miss Kiff says.

I freeze. It's not that I really care if I'm naked in front of these men. I just don't want to have to play the rest of the game without my dress on, which is what I assume is the item he'll ask me to remove. I only have two items of clothing on—my panties and the dress. The low-cut front leaves no room for a bra.

Mullock studies me a moment, once again encircling me.

"If you want me to remove the dress, then you're going to have to unzip me."

"Your panties," he says, shocking me.

The crowd boos.

I'm thankful as I shimmy my g-string down and then fling it in his direction.

"I don't want to be distracted looking at your ugly ass body," he mumbles under his breath.

I smile and shake my head.

Mullock walks over and picks up the whip before Ms. Kiff even finishes her sentence. "And one lashing."

He whips the whip hard against my back before I have time to prepare. I stumble forward in my heels, but I refuse to show any more weakness. My body can't handle the sudden force, though, and I fall to my knees, my hands landing on the ground in front of me.

More snickers and catcalls as I finally stand up on my feet, watching Mr. Mullock and Miss Kiff walk off the stage.

As I scramble off, my cheeks flush even though I didn't have to do anything remotely embarrassing. I make it back to my seat before the next man takes the stage.

"I yield," he says before his punishment even starts.

"Me as well," the next man says.

I frown, realizing that may be how the games go. I may be one of the only people who will do any of the dares, debts.

The dealer begins shuffling the cards, and then he looks at me. "Would you like to keep your remaining card or trade it in?"

"Keep," I say, knowing it's a ten.

He deals me four more cards.

I pick them all up, reveling in the fact that they are all face cards. I don't read a single one. All I know is that my next bet is going to be a good one.

9

LANGSTON

I STARE at the men sitting around the table as the dealer gives us new cards. Three men now stare back at me after we lost one in the previous round.

Men.

Why are there only men in this game besides Liesel?

What didn't Phoenix tell us? What kind of trap did she set?

We both know this is a trap. That's the only reason Phoenix would tell us about it. She wants us to suffer since she blames us for her suffering.

I replay every conversation I've ever had with her. Every kiss. Every fuck. Every time I thought Rose was our child. I remember it all and realize how wrong I've been about Phoenix. How much I missed that I should have caught. I should have known that Rose was Liesel's and not Phoenix's. I think somewhere deep down, I did know.

What game is she playing? How badly does she want Liesel and I to suffer during these games? Did she just set them up just to ensure we endured complete agony? Are the others playing the game in on it? Are they all their employees, which is why they aren't doing any of the debts when they lose?

So many questions and no answers.

My eyes drift to Liesel across the room. She doesn't look back, but I can see the hairs rise on her arms. Her body stiffens at the feel of my gaze on her. She's worried that I can't handle seeing her in pain.

She's right. I fucking can't.

Seeing her suffer is worse than any torture I could ever physically endure. I'd rather die than see her in pain.

But she deserves the same right I do to try to get our kids back. We are both willing to lose everything to protect them, as it should be. I have to put my feelings aside for now, but I hope to hell that we get Rose back before I have to watch Liesel endure more.

I take my cards as the next round starts. I don't have a single face card, which means it's going to be hard for me to win. At least the tasks won't add up to anything difficult.

The three men I'm playing against are all middle or upper aged. They all have gray hair, a well-fed stomach, and don more riches on their tuxes, watches, and rings than most people will earn in a lifetime.

I don't look at what the dares are on my cards. I don't care the pain I have to endure, as long as it doesn't hurt Liesel.

I smirk, thinking about my girl.

She might even slightly enjoy seeing me in pain for all the shit I've put her through over the years.

When it's my turn, I bet everything in my hand. "Twenty-three."

It's not enough. Every bet after mine is higher. It's my turn again, so I just lay my cards down, surrendering to the pain that I'm about to go through.

I look over at Liesel, who lets out a triumphant exhale. *Thank god her cards were better this time.*

A woman stands over me. "Mr. Pearce, right this way, please."

I stand up and follow her, my eyes still on Liesel. Her eyes grow wide, the corner of her mouth turns down, and the pink from her cheeks whitens. *Maybe I was wrong thinking that Liesel could somehow enjoy seeing me in pain, seeing another woman or man touch me? Maybe she feels more for me than I think? Maybe she already loves me?*

I walk onto the small stage, and the crowd grows silent, ready to watch the show. No one else is in line to the stage; the losers from the other tables walked right out of the room after they lost.

I'm right in thinking that only Liesel and I will be completing the debts. Only the two of us have enough at stake in order to be humiliated and in pain like this. For everyone else, this is just a silly game or an evil trap.

I find Liesel once again and give her a tight smile, trying to reassure her. I don't know what is about to happen because I didn't read the cards, but the only thing they could do to me that would truly hurt is attack Liesel or my kids. Since none of them are on the stage, the pain will feel nothing worse than a bee sting.

I wink at her.

Her frown deepens.

I hear the woman speak, but I don't register the words. My entire world is focused on Liesel, on figuring out how to get her to love me. Not just so we can get the stupid treasure, but because I want her to love me. I was wrong to run from loving her all these years. We can handle the consequences. I'm not even sure if there will be consequences of loving her.

I feel my jacket being ripped from my body. My shirt goes next, and I'm standing shirtless in front of the room.

Liesel's eyes water.

Why would they water? I'm just shirtless.

Then, I feel it. Not the pain, but the oozing of blood on my back.

I wish there was a way I could tell Liesel not to worry. With her safe in the same room as me, all I feel is her. My eyes plead with her not to worry, but I can see the concern marked on her face all the same.

A woman steps in front of me. I'm shocked when her lips land on mine. All I can think is when Liesel kissed that man. I turned feral as I watched another man touch what is mine, and I see the same look in Liesel's eyes now.

My eyebrows shoot up and wiggle in her direction. *I'm yours*, I remind her.

Liesel rolls her eyes at my antics, but then her face turns red. Her eyes almost come out of her head, and it looks like she's losing her mind as the woman licks her way down my body, groping me like her plaything.

I smirk, not because my body registers anything this woman is doing as remotely sexy, but because Liesel is jealous. I can work with jealous. Jealous can turn into love.

I hate you, I mouth to Liesel.

I hate you, too, she mouths back.

The woman who was licking my chest like her favorite lollipop grabs my chin and looks me in the eye. It's clear from the gleam in her eye that she's enjoying herself.

"I'm a sadist. I love this shit," she says as if there was any need to explain. Literal drool drips down her chin.

Her eyes look up at me as her tongue trails down my chest once again. "You sure you don't want to quit?"

Her hand rests on the top of my pants. It doesn't take much speculation on my part to guess what she's going to do next.

"I won't quit, no matter what you do to me. I can't."

Her eyes widen in realization. "The kid's yours."

I frown, my hand grabbing the back of her neck without thinking. "You know where she is?"

"As much as I'd enjoy the pain you want to inflict on me, you better let me go before they throw you out."

I let her go.

"Where is she?" I ask through gritted teeth.

She shrugs. "She's being kept as the prize."

"The prize?"

"Whoever wins gets her…"

They are trying to use my daughter as a prize for winning a fucked up game.

I can't.

My head snaps to Liesel, trying to let her know how important it is for us to win. We both knew it was important before, but now we know for sure. If we lose, Rose will be given to one of these men.

My heart.

I can't think about…

I just can't.

We have to win.

"Who—who are these men?"

"Most work for the Browns. The others are worse."

And then I feel her gripping my cock. I don't give a shit what she does. She can rip my cock from my body all I care.

Rose.

Atlas.

Declan.

We can't fail.

We won't fail.

If we fail, we have to fight to the death to get them back.

My eyes lock on Liesel, and her jealousy vanishes. She's no longer concerned that a sadistic woman is doing god knows what to my cock right now. She realizes why there are only men here—sick men who want our daughter.

Phoenix and her family were hurt more than we thought, and she plans on making us pay. All of these men know who we are, and they are going to do everything they can to destroy us, to hurt us. Humiliating us on this flimsy stage is the least of what they plan on doing.

They don't know who we are, though. There may be doubt about whether Liesel and I truly love each other, but there is no doubt that we love our children. They don't know the depths we will go to to protect them.

They're about to find out.

10

SIREN

I DON'T KNOW how I didn't realize it before, but in a flash, a flip in my mind switches, and I realize what's happening.

Why there are only men in the room playing the game.

Why Zeke and I are the only ones completing the bets.

Why it's us versus them.

Atlas is the prize.

If we fail...no, there is no failing.

I felt that before, but I feel it even stronger now.

We won't lose. We won't back down. Even if the game is purposefully rigged against us, it won't stop us.

Langston may feel like I betrayed him before, but every-thing I did was out of love for him. He's like a brother to me, same to Zeke. We will do whatever it takes to keep his child safe.

That's what keeps me going round after round.

It's what keeps me walking up on the shady stage that feels like it will collapse under my feet every time I take a step. It's what keeps me removing clothing item after clothing item until I'm naked in front of a room full of men. Until I've bled all I can. Until I no longer feel humiliated from their stares and chuckles. Until I've given up all of myself.

It's a small sacrifice if it means I get to save an innocent child.

I look over at Zeke, who is now seated at the same table as me.

There are only three of us left: Zeke, me, and a man in a suit who miraculously has never lost a single hand. Zeke and I seem to lose every round, and with each one, more blood and clothes.

Zeke stares back at me with a heaviness. He's calmer than I've ever seen him as he sits naked except for dried blood. His blood coats his skin, his beard, his hair. There are gashes all over his body from being whipped, beaten, tortured. Pain should be oozing off his body in waves; it should be all I feel from him. Instead, he feels as calm as the ocean after a storm —my steady hulk of a man.

I smile with newfound determination in my eyes. This man that I chose to spend my life with, that I love with everything in my being, is proving once again that he will fight by my side no matter what atrocities we face. Somehow, Zeke has me falling for him all over again.

I've never met a braver man.

A stronger one.

A more selfless one.

I know how hard this is for him, watching me get hurt and not doing anything. Yet, I can see in the tenseness of his muscles that he's always ready to fight. One move too far from one of these goons, and he'll spring into action, sacrificing himself to save me.

If we die, we die together. We die protecting an innocent child who is loved by us just as much we love our own child.

I wish we didn't live in a world filled with so much evil. But I can understand the pain of a woman who lost the love of her life and her children. Just thinking about losing Zeke or Atlas in this game has me spiraling into a place I can't even think about.

How cruel would I be to anyone who took everything I loved away from me? As inhumanly as humanly possible. I would turn into a hurricane destroying everything in my path. I wouldn't be able to see past my hate because if I let it go for a second, the loss would overwhelm me. I would have no choice but to hate.

I can understand why Phoenix wants to hurt us and anyone associated with anyone who took so much from her.

I can understand, but it's why I'm willing to fight so hard to not lose those I love. I know who and what I would become if I did—a monster.

I nod to Zeke as I sit next to him.

It's time to end this.

Our cards are dealt between the three of us. At the start, it was everyone against us, but we prevailed, and now we have the upper-hand. We outnumber him.

I look at my cards. For a while, I didn't even read the dares. It didn't matter what the cards said. I would do whatever it takes to win.

But one look at Zeke, and I realized it mattered. If I won a hand, I would spare Zeke from having to see me tortured or undressed.

This is the final round.

Either Zeke or I win, or they do.

I see several face cards, and I see a new card I haven't seen before.

I hold that card closer to my face and read slowly.

To win, you must sacrifice a part of yourself—your voice. Play the card, sacrifice yourself, and you win.

. . .

I look over at Zeke. His head is buried in one of his cards as he studies it closer, reading the words over and over. He has a version of this card too. The other man must have a similar card too, but we already know he won't play it.

Give up my voice? What does that even mean?

My heart races, thundering rapidly like a drum pounding through my body.

What does Zeke have to give up?

What do we do?

The game begins as usual.

The other man at our table has higher cards. I'm out of anything but the sacrifice card. I look to Zeke, and from his gaze, it seems he's in the same position.

We have to win.

There is nothing left to do but sacrifice everything. We both play our cards and hope to hell it's enough to save Atlas.

11

BECKETT

FINALLY, I've made it to the last table.

It's down to two—me and Corbin.

I was surprised he showed his face, even more surprised to see that he entered the game. And he, unlike the rest of his minions entered in the game, even did one of the dares he bet. It cost him his pretty face getting marred, swollen, and bloodied up.

It's that same face now that's dripping with blood that stands between me and saving Declan. He's the one remaining wall to possibly earning forgiveness for losing Rose and Atlas—not that I'll ever be able to forgive myself.

I'll win.

It's not about having the cards. It's about willing to bet everything. It's about being willing to endure the most pain, suffer the most without fear. That's how you win this game.

That's something I have plenty of. Losing an arm will teach you a thing or two about pain.

My concern isn't about how much more I can endure. Sure, there is blood dripping down my forehead and seeping into my eye, making it hard to see. And yes, my ears are ringing and haven't stopped for hours now. I have gashes all over my back. My cock doesn't want to be touched ever again. I'm pretty sure I can't have children after the beating my balls took.

But that's nothing.

My concern is what happens after I win. *Will I actually get Declan? Or is Corbin not going to keep his promise? Is he going to find a way to disqualify me? Is this all a ruse to keep us at specific locations while they move the kids to someplace we will never find them?*

The only way to find out is to finish the game.

Cards are dealt one by one to Corbin and me.

Neither of us looks at the cards. We glare at each other like this is a staring contest instead of a fucked up game where lives are hanging in the balance.

Finally, we both pick up our cards one by one. I have a few face cards, a two, and an ace. Then I pick up the last card.

This one is different than any of the cards I've previously gotten. 'Sacrifice Card' is written across the top.

I don't always read the bets, knowing there is nothing I wouldn't do to rescue Declan, but this card I read.

To win, you must sacrifice a part of yourself—your ability to feel and touch. Play the card, sacrifice yourself, and you win.

I look up at Corbin, who is grinning at me wickedly. No doubt he doesn't have a sacrifice card. That's what this has all been about—making us do the most ridiculous things, show how terribly we are suffering, then really make us hurt.

I'm afraid it's a trick. Even if we win, the kids might not

simply be returned to us like they say. *What choice do I have, though?*

Corbin bets, then it's my turn.

I immediately go all in, including the sacrifice card. I'm tired of the games.

I either win and get Declan, or I lose and fight this motherfucker to the death. Either way is fine with me because either way, I'll win. I don't accept defeat.

I smirk at Corbin as I go all in, and his eyebrows jump up a second in shock. He didn't think I'd play the sacrifice card. He didn't think I'd be willing to go that far. He thinks pain scares me. He has no idea that losing my family is the only thing that scares me.

My ability to feel and touch—I'm not sure what that means, but I've lost a limb already. I can handle losing any physical part of my body. I have no problem adapting. Whatever it means, I'll give it up.

"Your loss," Corbin says.

"As long as I get the kid, I don't care what you do to me."

12

LIESEL

"I HATE YOU," I say as I stand in the center of the stage, looking out at Langston.

The crowd chuckles, thinking I truly hate Langston. That couldn't be further from the truth. Even when I hated him, I still loved him. He's a drug I can't give up.

Right now, I wish he hated me. He could ruin everything if he prevents my sacrifice.

His limits have been pushed about what he can handle me enduring and what he can't. So far, he's stayed on the sidelines watching but not trying to stop the price I had to pay for losing each round.

I've seen every vein in his head pop, I've seen his muscles flex with the need to step in, I've seen his face redden as he held his breath to keep his ass in his seat instead of throwing me over his shoulder and getting me the fuck out of here.

This round will test him more than I think he can handle.

I'm standing naked on the little stage. I lost my clothes after the last round, as did Langston.

Anyone else standing in my place might be trembling in fear. Goosebumps would have surely formed. Their hearts would have sped to an ungodly speed or slowed beyond detection.

For me, the only thing my body feels is Langston all the way across the room. His eyes sparkle with his love even from there. *How foolish was I to try and stop us from loving each other all these years? Why did I let him hate me? Why not demand his love all those years ago when we were five years old?*

Would we still be here now? About to lose everything to try and save our children?

Maybe, but at least if we'd spent those years loving each other, it wouldn't feel like we wasted so much time now.

I feel a hand start to graze my body, and Langston's body changes in the familiar way. His lips thin, his hand twitches, his eyes glaze over into darkness. He's fighting every nerve in his body to not save me. Saving me means losing Rose, and our kids will always come first.

"Stay," I half mouth, half say to Langston.

Another hand touches me. I try not to focus or think about where. It's easy to tune out when I'm so focused on not showing any signs of distress to Langston. I don't want him to suffer because he thinks I'm in pain—I'm not.

The debt I lost said that any man in this room could touch me where they want. So far, I've been poked and prodded everywhere—places no one but Langston deserves to touch. But the hand we've been dealt means we have to fight to get to that place. And when we do, I have a feeling our happily ever after is going to be short-lived. Even if we find happiness together, something will come along and take it away. The world always takes from us. It's why I've been so opposed to us being together.

I feel the man slide his grubby finger inside me. I don't react. I'm not in pain, not really. This will all be over soon, so fucking soon.

Langston looks like he's about to combust. But if I could

stay in my chair while that sadistic woman almost cut off all the blood supply to his balls, then he can sit in his chair for this.

Langston can't put up with it, though. He rushes onto the stage. The man who was fingering me steps back, probably because he thinks Langston will punch him. Langston takes a deep breath as he stands in front of me, shielding me from the rest of the men.

"Langston, I'm okay. I promise," I say, making my voice sound as strong as possible.

"I know you are. I'm not."

"We have to play the game. We have to win. There is no other option."

"I know."

"Then, what are you doing? Go back to your chair."

He tilts his head as cocky grin spreads. "I'm having my turn."

I frown, confused, just before his hand cups my sex.

"Oh."

I bite my lip to keep the sex noises that are begging to leave my body as Langston rubs a thumb around my clit before slowly pushing a finger inside of me.

God, it feels like no other man. I could be blindfolded and fucked in the exact same way by every man here, and I'd be able to tell the difference between Langston and everyone else. He may have just recently become my husband, but he's been my everything for so much longer.

My breath speeds up as he touches me. My cheeks flush, and my toes curl on the stage.

I prepare myself for the inevitable—someone is going to yank him off of me.

Langston leans into my body, his lips resting on mine. My eyes are closed as the pressure builds inside me. My mind begins to soar above all the wickedness of the room.

Vile creatures walk among us every day, only to haunt our dreams later. I float above it all.

"Come, my wife."

I do.

Langston's mouth closes over mine, keeping all of my noises to himself. His body blocks the crowd so they can't see my face as I come apart, as Langston claims me in front of everyone while protecting me in the only way he can.

"They can touch you all they want, but you're mine," he says loud enough for the whole room to hear.

"Leave," I breathe out.

"What?"

"Thank you. I hate you. Now, leave. It's easier for both of us. Go take a break in the bathroom or grab a drink at the bar."

He frowns.

It's my turn to help him.

He doesn't like it, but eventually, he walks out of the room.

I exhale, feeling a weight lift from me.

More touching me, defiling me, trying to make a claim on me, but all I feel is Langston. His touch still tingles everywhere, and when they touch me, it ignites his touch once again.

I don't know how much time passes. I'm blissfully ignorant to it all until Kiff finally tells me I can step down.

One step, then two, then…

I fall.

The room breaks out into laughter.

I don't care.

My head spins. I must have gotten lightheaded from how long I was standing upright.

"We are going to take a twenty-minute break and then start the next round of games," the host says.

Twenty-minute break.

My stomach heaves, and I know how I'm going to be spending my time.

I force myself up before I race to the bathroom.

I clutch the toilet as I dry heave. My stomach churns, but nothing comes out. Sweat forms and mixes with the blood seeping from my wounds before making a small puddle on the floor underneath me.

I expect Langston will burst through the stall door at any moment. This is the women's bathroom, but that wouldn't stop him. I expect him to search me out the second he realizes there is a break.

He can't find me here. He can't find me crumpled on the bathroom floor, a complete mess.

I flush the toilet and then use the seat to push myself up. My feet wobble, and the world spins around my head. I hold my arms out by my sides, trying to keep my balance. They flail a bit as I walk over to the sink and wash my hands. I try to wash some of the blood and sweat from my body, but it's no use. All it does is smear.

I decide to focus my attention on my face, thinking I can at least wash enough off, so my eyes no longer sting.

"I said macaroni and cheese, not cheese pizza," a soft voice says.

I turn the water off, my ears perk up, and my eyes search the three stalled bathroom for the source of the voice.

I throw open each of the stalls, but the room is empty.

Speak again, I beg the silence.

Did I just imagine that sweet little voice in my head?

"You are so incompetent. When I get older, I'm going to get you fired," the sassy voice says again.

I grin as I look up at the vent directly above me.

Rose.

She's here.

Right above me.

My heart flutters, coming alive again with true hope I didn't know I could feel anymore. Rose is here. She's alive, and from the sound of her voice, it sounds like she's giving them hell.

This all won't be for nothing. We will be able to get her back. *Maybe sooner than we think?*

I consider my options to get to Rose. Leave the bathroom, find the stairs, count the doors to her room, and then try to sneak in. That's a lot of things that would have to go perfectly for me to be able to find her.

Or?

Or I climb up through the vent.

My time to make a move is running out. We only had a twenty-minute break. This could all fail miserably, but my gut tells me I have to try.

I can still hear Rose's voice, but it's softer now. I can't make out her words.

I have to try.

I run to one of the stalls and climb up on the toilet. I look around for my next move and decide the best option is to climb up onto the wall of the stall. I stand on my tiptoes, barely able to reach the top of the wall while I balance on the top of the toilet.

I grab hold of the top of the stall, and then I clamber up. I slip and slide, but somehow I manage to hang on until I can hike my leg up onto the top of the wall.

The ceiling is tiled, so I push up on one of the tiles. It pops open. I grab onto the cheap ceiling tile and toss it to the floor. Finally, I pull myself up into the opening.

I take a deep breath. Climbing up into the ceiling won't help if I can't get into the ducts and up to the floor above me.

I crawl across the ceiling to the vent I saw. When I get to it, I pop the opening off before sliding up inside. I hold myself up with my arms and legs bracing against the sides of vents.

"I asked for milk, not soda," Rose says.

"We don't have milk," a man's voice grumbles back, clearly annoyed.

I smile. Rose has this man wrapped around her finger.

"The least you could get me is water. Soda is so unhealthy."

"Fine. I'll get your damn water. I'll be right back."

He's leaving.

My eyes widen, and my heart pounds. This is my chance.

I scramble up as fast as I can until I get to the top of the vent that leads into the room where she's being held. The lid is stuck. I push as hard as I can, but it won't budge.

"Rose," I whisper through the vent.

"Who is that?" she asks.

"I'm a friend of your dad's. I'm Liesel."

Her eyes peer down at me through the slats.

"Liesel? That's a funny name."

I smile at how truthful she is. She's not afraid to speak her mind.

"It is, isn't it? I wish we had time to talk more, but I'm here to take you back to your dad."

"Thank god. These people are idiots."

I laugh.

"Rose, can you help me try to get the top of this vent off before that man comes back?"

She nods and kneels down, her small hands gripping the edge of the vent cover while I push up.

It starts to budge.

"Almost there," I say, pushing with everything I have.

It pops open, and I'm face to face with my daughter. I'm bloodied, naked, and my head is peering out from the top of a floor vent. Of all the ways I imagined meeting my daughter, this isn't one of them. And yet, seeing her smile at me like I'm her savior makes it all worthwhile. Seeing that she isn't injured or hurt is the miracle I've been praying for.

"Why are you covered in blood?" she asks.

"I'll tell you someday, but for now, we have to go."

She nods.

I hold out my arms, and to my surprise, she lowers herself into my arms, no questions asked. She's either very naive or a good judge of character. Carefully, I lower us down into the vent, then I pull the lid back so, hopefully, her guard won't realize how she escaped.

Then I help her down the vent.

I carry her down until the duct turns, and then she can start crawling on her own. She's much faster than I am. I see stars when I open my eyes, and my muscles shake with each movement. I'm naked; I have no weapons, nothing to get her out of here. This was a terrible idea.

"Rose, wait a sec," I say.

She stops. Her head looks back at me as her blonde curls hang down her back.

"I need you to listen to me carefully, Rose."

"Okay," she says quietly.

"I have to go back to where I came from now. I have to tell your father where to find you."

"You're not coming with?"

"Not right away. I'll meet up with you both later, but I need you to keep crawling as quietly as you can in the ducts here. You can go straight or to the right, but try not to go to the left or back the way we came unless you have no other choice. Your dad will know where to look for you."

She nods slowly, her eyes big and yet so strong. She's the strongest little girl I've ever seen.

I smile at her, trying to reassure her. "You've got this.

Your dad is the smartest man in the whole world. He'll find you no matter which way you go."

My hand reaches out before I realize what I'm doing. Her small hand reaches back, and I give it a squeeze of encouragement. Or maybe she's giving me encouragement. Either way, touching her small hand flips a switch inside me. I thought I was protective of my kids before. But now, there is nothing that will stop me.

"You've got this, Rose. Trust your instincts and try to be quiet as a mouse."

"Mice aren't quiet," she laughs.

I chuckle. "I'll see you soon, Rose. And your dad will find you sooner."

I wink and then watch as she starts crawling again before I turn around and head back to the bathroom.

I'm not as graceful returning to the bathroom as I was climbing up. I fall to the floor.

"Ow," I say, trying to rub my sore neck as I get back onto my feet.

Quickly, I run out of the bathroom, hoping I run into Langston before the next round starts. As I exit, I see the other men walking leisurely back into the game room. My time is up.

I head to the entrance and poke my head inside, but I don't see Langston.

"Where have you been?" Langston says from behind me.

I exhale, my eyes closing in relief.

I turn and face him as his eyes search mine, trying to understand why he couldn't find me for the last twenty minutes.

"Lose the next game. Don't complete the debt," I say as quietly as I can between clenched teeth. Hoping to god no one else hears me.

"Why?" he asks.

"If you will all take your seats, the game will resume."

"Search the ducts on the east side. I'll keep playing and give you as much time as I can."

Then I turn and head inside, hoping Langston got my message loud and clear.

13

LANGSTON

THE DUCTS?

What the hell?

Liesel walks away from me back into the room. I follow after her calmly, even though I actually want to run after her and force her to tell me what the hell that was all about.

I don't have too much time to think about it before I'm sitting back at the table, and cards are being dealt out again.

There are only two other players left at my table. We are nearing the point where they will combine us all to one table.

I glance at my hand. It's mediocre at best—one face card and the rest in the single digits.

Liesel wants me to lose on purpose and then quit when I get to the stage. She wants me to look in the ducts on the east side of the building.

Why?

Did she find where they are holding Rose? If so, what do the ducts have to do with it? Is that the only way to get to the room where they are holding Rose? Or is this some elaborate way to convince me to quit so she doesn't have to see me in pain anymore?

I peer at Liesel over the top of my cards at the next table. She is looking right at me, not bothering to look at her own cards. Her eyes are wild and desperate.

Trust me, she mouths.

Trust her.

I close my eyes, trying to listen with my heart. My heart wants me to throw Liesel over my shoulder and run as far away from this place as my feet will take us. My heart wants me to save Liesel and then find another way to save Rose.

Trust her.

I love Liesel. I know that. Part of loving her means trusting her. It's not something I'm good at, but if I love her, maybe I should start trying.

I'm the first at my table to bet. I bet everything, which only gets me to nineteen points. It won't be enough.

It's not.

Liesel wins her hand, knocking another person out of her table.

My eyes lock with hers as I stand up and walk to the stage area. They never leave hers. That's not unusual; my eyes are always on hers when I'm suffering.

This time is different, though. This time I look at her to make sure she hasn't lost her damn mind. Or she's not trying to sacrifice herself to save me. I look for any sign that she's changed her mind.

But she looks completely at peace when she sees that I'm going to do what she asks.

I don't know what my dares are, but I feel a slash land on my already ripped apart back. I usually try to keep the pain inside, but this time I let out the wince. Then another, louder groan with the second beating.

I fall to my knees on the third.

The fourth—tears are falling down my face.

And by the fifth, I'm holding my hand up in surrender.

The room gasps as I give up, collapsing in a heap on the floor, completely defeated.

The room is silently watching and judging me. Then they turn their attention to Liesel. I lift my head enough to see tears falling down her face.

Drip.

Drip.

Drip.

Each drip is a mark on my soul. I feel like I failed her, even though I'm doing what she says she wants.

The room may think the tears burning down her cheeks are a sign of defeat, fear, and heartbreak.

Only I can see the truth behind the tears. I see the absolute relief and the hint of a smile she holds back, so the others don't get suspicious.

Eventually, I'm lifted onto my feet by two men. I'm walked off the stage and led out of the room, away from Liesel.

That's when my heart starts losing its shit. I just left her in a room full of dangerous men to fend for herself while I go in search of our daughter that she thinks I'll be able to find if I use the ducts. Liesel's lost it. *What the hell was I thinking leaving her?*

I should go back, change my mind. I can't leave her.

The men continue to drag me by my arms. I don't know where they are taking me; I just know they need to turn around and take me back to Liesel.

Suddenly, I'm falling face-first onto a tiled floor. I catch myself at the last second.

"Here, clean yourself and get dressed. You can either wait in the bar, or we can call you a car ride home," one of the men says before the door swings shut.

I realize I'm in a bathroom, and the heap of fabric that was tossed at me is a towel, pants, and shirt.

I quickly stand up and use the towel to wipe some of the blood off. Without a shower and closing some of my wounds, nothing will get rid of the blood.

I put the plain clothes on. They are a little big, but the pants stay up when I walk, so they're good enough. Then I go in search of the ducts on the east side of the building. I'm not sure exactly what I'm going to find, but I hope I find Rose. Rose is the only thing that would be worth me leaving Liesel alone in that room.

I exit the bathroom and assume those idiot guards are going to be waiting for me. They aren't.

There is no one in the hallway.

I glance up, sure that there are cameras monitoring me. People who work for the Browns are watching me and will attack me if I go somewhere undesired.

I move quickly, headed toward the east side of the building. My ears perk up, and my eyes glance around every turn, trying to figure out where Rose might be.

The ducts?

Rose must be a floor above us, but still, *why would Liesel tell me to search the ducts? Is that the only way to get to the second floor?*

There is another bathroom on this side, so I decide to duck inside, hoping there aren't any cameras in here while I figure out a plan.

I pace inside, trying to figure out what Liesel isn't telling me.

I hear a clank, and I look up.

"Shit," a soft voice curses through the vent.

My heart—my heart leaps at that sound, a sound I wasn't sure I'd ever hear again. My precious girl is in the ducts.

"Rose?" I say hesitantly.

"Dad?" her voice returns.

Oh my god.

The ceiling is low, so I jump with everything I have and grab hold of the vent cover. It falls off easily with my weight. Then I jump again and pull myself up the sides of the vent. I poke my head inside to see my favorite smile in the whole world staring back at me.

"You came for me, just like the woman with the funny name said you would."

I smile. I don't think I'll ever stop smiling.

"Liesel?"

She nods.

"Did she help you get in the ducts?"

"Yes, she told me to crawl straight or right, not left. To be as quiet as possible and that you would find me. I'm so glad you did."

"Me too."

I feel myself slipping. I can't hang on much longer.

"Rose, I'm going to drop back down. After I do, I'm going to need you to jump down, and I'll catch you. Can you do that?" I already know my adventurous girl will have no problem jumping.

"Of course, I can do that," she says in her sassy little voice.

I let go and land back on my feet.

"Okay, Rose, I'm ready."

I watch as her feet scoot to the opening, and then she falls down into my arms.

I squeeze her tight to me the second she lands in my arms. I'm never letting her go again. I hold her tighter against my body.

"Dad, you're squeezing too hard."

I chuckle, but don't let her go. Based on how tightly she's squeezing back, I don't think she wants me to let her go.

Liesel found her. She protected her. She knew she couldn't get Rose out of here safely on her own, so she sacrificed herself to ensure Rose and I could escape.

How could I have ever hated Liesel or thought she was a monster?

"I need you to climb onto my back, Rose."

She nods, and I help her onto my back.

I don't have a gun or any other weapon, but that won't stop me from getting Rose out of here.

A part of my heart grieves as I leave Liesel behind, though. It's the right thing to do. Liesel chose to make this sacrifice, but it feels wrong to leave her behind for any amount of time.

"I'll come back for you," I whisper, and then I get Rose out of this hell hole.

1 4

LIESEL

THERE'S a shift in the air. Goosebumps form on my arms. My heart stops. My breathing slows. The world changes for the better.

I purse my lips and let out a long exhale as my entire body relaxes.

Langston found Rose.

"If you will all move to the table in the center," the hose says.

There are only three of us left, so we're moved to the final table.

Rose is safe.

But what about the others?

I thought I only had one child to worry about, but now I know I'm a mother of three. My heart is split three ways, trying to ensure they are all safe. I'm not going to survive worrying about all of them.

I wish I had a better connection to them so I would be able to feel the shift like I did when Langston found Rose. The only reason I felt it is because of my connection to Langston, not my connection to my children.

Our dealer starts handing out cards, and I try to focus. It doesn't matter now if I win or lose, but I need to protect Rose and Langston by giving them as much time as possible to get away. And if I win, they'll have no reason to go after her. She would belong to me either way.

So I'll win—to protect her.

Whatever pain they want me to endure now is nothing compared to the pain I've felt in my lifetime. Now that Rose and Langston are safe, there is nothing they could do to me here that could hurt me.

Cards are dealt one by one, and I feel an icy chill curl around my spine, taking hold. I stare at the extra card that was passed out. *Why is there an extra card?*

I hesitate to pick up the cards, knowing that whatever is on that card is about to change my fate once again. For once, I'm desperate to know what my own future holds.

The other two men at my table have both picked up their cards. They scan them quickly before staring me down, trying to intimidate me.

I've come this far. I won't be intimidated.

I grab the cards and slide them toward me before picking them up. I scan the first five cards quickly before getting to the new card—the card that will change everything, as usual, with my life.

'The Sacrifice Card' the top reads.

I smile; how ironic. My whole life is one big sacrifice. My life has never been my own. First, it was about protecting Langston. Then, it became about saving my kids. And after this is all over, it will always be about Langston and my kids. That is my entire purpose for living—to protect them.

I read the card quickly, knowing it doesn't matter what the words say. I'll do whatever it takes to protect those I love. I always have.

The words sink in. They envelop my body. The sacrifice I will have to make. It's the same one I always make.

The first two men bet.

I look down at my cards. Without the sacrifice card, I'll lose. I can't lose, so I do the only thing I can. I sacrifice everything to protect those I love.

LANGSTON

I GOT ROSE OUT. I only had to punch a couple of guys and shoot another, but I got her out. I was afraid she'd be traumatized when she saw me with a gun. Instead, she beamed like I was a freaking superhero or something.

I don't deserve her. I don't deserve any of my kids. Still, once this is all over, I'm taking them somewhere safe. I'm quitting the business. I don't want to have to look over my shoulder every day for the rest of my life wondering if today is my last day or not. My kids deserve better.

Enzo met me about thirty minutes after I left. Thank god, he'd been monitoring my location and started driving as soon as he saw us leaving. He took Rose somewhere safe. She fell asleep as soon as I put her in his arms. I don't know what she's been through, but she looks physically safe. *Psychologically, who knows what she went through?* She's tough, though, and I'll do everything I can to help her heal and move on from this.

Until I can get back, I trust Enzo and Kai to keep Rose safe and to keep her away from Phoenix. I don't know what we are going to tell Rose and Atlas about Phoenix, but for now, keeping them away is for the best.

Now, I'm driving like a maniac to get back to Liesel, to get her the fuck out of there.

I run every red light. Take every turn too sharp. Speed as fast as the car will go through the straightaways. But none of it is fast enough. Every second that I'm away is another second of pain for Liesel. Another second of agony that she has to heal from. Another second something could happen that she won't be able to get over. It's another second of me hating myself. Another second that could be our last together.

A tear springs to my eye just thinking about life without Liesel. Our entire life has been about each other. I can't lose her now that I've finally gotten her. Now that I'm so close to getting her to love me like we should have all those years ago before life fucked us both.

I slam on the breaks as I pull back up at the club. I open my door and jump out, running to the entrance. Nothing can stop me now, except…

"Liesel."

She's standing in the doorway in gray sweatpants and a loose-fitting white T-shirt, an angel casually walking away from hell. Blood clings to her skin, littered with cuts and bruises. She actually doesn't look much, if any, worse than the last time I saw her.

And she's alive.

She's free.

She's mine.

I pause for a second before my brain works again, and I race to her. I force myself to stop just in front of her, my hands reaching out but not touching her. Just because I don't see any new injuries doesn't mean she wasn't hurt worse.

And it doesn't mean the injuries I saw happen don't still hurt like hell. I won't make her suffer more.

"You got Rose?" she asks.

I nod.

A happy tear rolls down her cheek as she smiles and then jumps into my embrace.

Once she's in my arms, I can't help but hold her tightly. My arms extend around her and hold onto her like vice grips. I'm never letting any part of my family go again —never.

Her head nestles into my chest, and her tears soak through my shirt.

"We need to leave," I say, wanting to get her as far away from this vile place as I can. Once we are safely away, we can talk more.

She nods as I lead her to my car. We both jump in, and I drive just as hard and fast as I did to get back to her. My hand finds hers, and we hold hands, not speaking, letting the car engine do all the talking.

After speeding away and seeing no cars following us, I pull over into an alleyway and park the car.

Then I look over at Liesel.

"What happened?" I ask.

She shrugs. "I won the game. I told them I had already taken my prize and then I left. They have no reason to come after Rose now. I won."

I nod. There's a heaviness in her eyes. *What isn't she telling me?*

"Rose is safe with Enzo and Kai. I didn't see any injuries, and her spirit hasn't changed. I don't think they hurt her."

"Thank god."

I grab the base of her neck and rub my thumb over her swollen cheek. I want to know everything that happened, and yet I'm not sure my heart can take it. She can't keep putting herself last. She can't keep taking all the pain while shielding the rest of us. She has to let some of us take on the danger too.

I'm about to ask her more questions when my phone buzzes in my pocket.

I can feel Liesel's heartbeat in her neck skip when I reach for my phone.

"It's Siren," I say before I answer. "Hello."

Liesel grips onto my hand so tight that my knuckles start turning white.

"Hey," Zeke says.

"Did you win the game? Did you get Atlas?"

There's a long pause. Too long of a pause.

"What did they say?" Liesel asks.

I shake my head. "Zeke? Siren?"

I hold the phone out, thinking that the call must have dropped, but it still shows that we are connected.

"We won the game. We got Atlas," Zeke says, his voice sounds strange when he should sound happy.

"Good, let's all go to my island house. Meet there. We can protect ourselves there." I look to Liesel, who nods her head in agreement.

Another long pause before Zeke answers. "See you there soon."

The call ends. That was strange.

"Atlas is safe?" Liesel asks.

"Atlas is safe."

More tears water her eyes as she almost collapses with relief against me.

Two down, one to go.

We are back to where we started.

"I—"

Another phone call.

We both stare down at my phone in disbelief as Beckett calls me.

Our hearts thump in unison. This could be the call that changes everything. The call that means we finally have all of our kids.

"Didyouwin? DoyouhaveDeclan?" I ask, rushing my words out so quickly I'm not even sure Beckett can understand me.

"I won—"

"Thank god, meet us at my island house. Okay?"

The line cuts out, but it doesn't matter. I blink back my own tears, but there is no use. For the first time, all three of Liesel's kids are safe and on their way to meet her.

"He's safe?"

I nod, grabbing her cheeks and resting my forehead against hers. "They all are."

Our tears mix together, as do our smiles and laughs. Too many happy emotions flood through us. I can't remember another time when I've been this happy.

"What does this mean? What do we have to do?" Liesel asks, completely dumbfounded.

"It means we're safe. We'll make sure Corbin and the rest of them are no longer a threat, but it's over. We are safe. We won. It means we only have to keep pursuing the treasure if you want to. If you don't, we can tell people we found it, and it was only a million dollars or something; not worth anyone coming after us. No one will know. We're safe. I won't let anyone hurt you or our kids ever again."

Her lips slam down on mine as I say my last word.

I groan into her lips, partly because moving fucking hurts, but more because she tastes so damn delicious. I've wanted to kiss her every second since we started all of this. And now—now it feels like we can finally kiss, fuck, be together in every way. There is nothing stopping us now, not anymore.

I run my hand under her shirt, needing to feel her skin. I stop when she moans as my fingertips encounter the sticky warmth of her blood.

"I'm sorry. I didn't mean to hurt you. I—"

"Shut up." She grabs my face, stares down at me, and starts climbing across the seat toward me. "You didn't hurt me. You couldn't hurt me. When you touch me, all I feel is mind-blowing pleasure. You overwhelm me, Langston. Now hate fuck me like you want to." She rips her shirt off her body, revealing too many bruises, cuts, and blood stuck to her skin.

My eyes sadden.

"Hate fuck me," she repeats, pushing her breasts into my face. Her hand tilts my head back while she pushes her nipple against my lips.

Hate fuck her?

I don't hate her; I love—oh, she wants me to make love to her. Hate means love. *How could I have forgotten?*

"My pleasure." I lick over her already hard nipple and am rewarded with soft, gentle moans. They're the kind that hits me straight in the groin, making me instantly hard.

She notices and rubs her sex against me through our clothes. I'm so wound up that I'm going to come way too quickly, which is probably a good thing considering we are in a cramped car in an alleyway and not entirely safe. Phoenix's people could find us here.

But it's not what Liesel deserves, and I plan on only giving her what she deserves from now on.

I take my time teasing her first nipple, then her second, careful to listen for any sound that I might be hurting her. She moans with every lick of my tongue, but now that I'm listening more carefully, I realize her moans are of pleasure.

I won't hurt her ever again. And I'll spend the rest of my life making up for all the hurt she's had to go through. And I'll start right now.

My fingers dive into her pants, between her folds, finding her clit as I tease her nipple with my tongue.

I rub over her sensitive nub in slow circles, knowing there is no way I'll fuck her until I've made her come. I don't know what torture she's just endured, but I want this to take it all away.

Her hands grab onto my shoulders, her eyes close, and her body shakes as I continue to bring her closer to ecstasy.

"I need you inside me," she whispers.

I slip a finger inside, pumping gently into her while my thumb circles her clit, moving faster, applying more pressure.

"That's not what—aww—I meant," she says as I slide two fingers inside her.

I kiss my way up the curve of her chest and neck until I can nip the edge of her earlobe with my teeth.

"I know," I growl.

She tremors at my words, and it pushes her into a spiral of pulses that race down her spine all the way to her toes. She climaxes hard on my fingers, soaking me and making me fall even harder for her as I watch her come so undone.

Liesel's body may be broken, but her soul is not. Her soul is more alive than ever. And I want it—her soul, her heart. I want it all.

Right now, she wants my cock. She's grabbing at my waistband, trying to push my pants down to get to me. When I don't immediately rush to help her, she snarls at me.

"Help me get these pants off you, now."

I grin at her bossiness, her neediness. I love it all.

I shove my pants down until they are a heap at my ankles. Before I have time to even stroke myself, she's already on top of and pushing down on my cock like she owns me, which I guess she does. I love that even more.

She starts sliding up and down on my cock. She's going to make me come way too soon, and all I can do is look up in her eyes, knowing that I want to look into her eyes every second of the rest of my life. For the first time, I feel like that's a real possibility.

"Stop looking at me and hate fuck me," she says, moving faster over my dick. I can tell it's exhausting her and that she wants me to take control soon.

I grab her hips and drive into her, keeping some restraint so I don't hurt her. The devil in her eyes tells me to fuck her harder. She doesn't want to be treated gingerly; she wants to be fucked hard.

The next stroke is harder. It rattles her body, but her moans only heighten. It drives me to fuck her rougher until I can't hold back any longer.

"I hate you," I moan as I come.

"I. Hate. You. Too," she screams as she comes on my cock.

We pant into each other's mouth; both of us still consumed by everything we just went through. Liesel eventually rests her head against my shoulder. She must be completely exhausted and starving.

I grab my phone and text out a quick message to Enzo, letting him know to get us a jet and that we are all flying to my place.

"Liesel, baby, as much as I want you, you have to get in your seat so I can drive."

"No," she says softly, wrapping her arms tighter around my neck.

I can't let her go either, even if I wanted to, so I don't. I hold her in my lap as I carefully pull back out on the road and start driving us to the airport.

I'll never let her go.

LIESEL

I FALL asleep against Langston's shoulder. I know sleeping on his lap while he drives isn't the safest thing, but I decided we might as well tempt fate after everything we've been through. For now, I just need to be with Langston to not overthink everything.

He says this is the end; everyone is safe.

I know the truth.

The end is when we can finally say, 'I love you.' It happens when we get a happily ever after or we die tragically.

We didn't say, 'I love you.' We didn't celebrate as one big happy family. And as far as I know, I'm not dead, *but who knows? Maybe I am, and I've died and gone to heaven?* That's what it feels like lying on Langston's shoulder.

What comes next, though?

Do I tell him everything that happened; how I won the game?

Do I finally get to stop hunting for the truth?

"Huntress, we're here," Langston says, kissing my forehead. He doesn't realize I'm already awake.

I open my eyes and smile at him. The sky is dark, but I spot the plane behind us.

Langston pops the door open and then lifts me out of the car. He carries me honeymoon style on the tarmac and then up the stairs to the private jet.

"Daddy!" Rose's voice screams happily as we walk into the plane's cabin.

I think Langston is going to set me down so he can scoop Rose up, but instead, he somehow scoops up Rose until she's lying on my lap. She gives Langston a big hug.

I can't hold back my own smile.

"Liesel!" she yells happily when she recognizes me and throws her little arms around my neck.

My first hug.

Thump, thump. Thump, thump.

All I can feel is the beat of her heart against mine. A strange, wonderful feeling I never thought I'd get to feel.

"Thank you for saving me," Rose says when she leans back.

"You did a pretty good job of that yourself, but gladly. I'd save you any time." I will save you every time.

Rose smiles brighter. "Good, I'd save you too."

I smile. "I know you would."

Her bright eyes look between Langston and me curiously. I don't know what she sees when she looks between us, but I can see the wheels turning in her head.

I give Langston a worried look. I'm not ready to tell Rose that I'm her biological mother. I'm not ready to tell her that we're married or make any commitment to stay in her life.

"Have you eaten, Rose bug?" Langston asks, trying to change the subject.

She nods. "But I could use dessert."

Langston laughs. "Let's see if we can find you dessert."

He sets her down and then puts my feet back on the

ground while keeping a hand at the small of my back. We both could use a shower, change of clothes, food, and sleep. But first, we need to take care of Rose.

We find Enzo and Kai sitting on one of the tan couches in the back of the plane. They both stand when we come back. Kai walks over to me. "You okay?" she asks quietly.

I give her a quick nod. "We'd be better if we found some dessert."

Kai smiles down at Rose. "We have a couple of different flavors of ice cream. Which is your favorite, Rose?"

She thinks really hard.

"How about one of everything?" I say.

Rose nods happily.

Kai winks. "One of everything coming right up."

Rose hops up on one of the couches. She seems completely normal, so I'm glad this doesn't seem to be phasing her.

"Where is Mom? Is she meeting us on the island like Atlas?"

The room quiets.

Langston halts mid-step. He looks to Enzo as he realizes that Phoenix could be hidden somewhere on this very plane.

"Your mom had an important job she had to do. I'm not sure if she'll be able to get away from work to come to the island or not," Enzo answers.

Well, at least that means Phoenix isn't on the plane, but I don't know what we do about Phoenix long term. Rose thinks Phoenix has been her mom her entire life. We can't kill Phoenix, but we can't just let her go back to being Rose's mother either.

Kai returns with a giant bowl of ice cream and several spoons.

Rose holds out her hands, and Kai places the bowl in her

lap. Rose's eyes light up so big when she sees the mountain of ice cream.

"Dad, Liesel, you need to help me eat this. It looks like you both have been starving like me," Rose says.

Langston and I exchange worried glances as we join Rose on the couch, taking a seat on either side of her. "Did they not feed you, the men who took you?" Langston asks casually as he takes one of the spoons and a bite to satisfy Rose and probably some of his own hunger.

"They tried to, but everything they kept feeding me was gross like a cold pizza and sodas. I know I'm not supposed to drink sodas, so I didn't drink any," she answers.

I laugh, my eyes meeting Langston's as we relax, knowing that Rose was at least offered food.

We all eat in comfortable silence for a little bit before I've had enough sweets in my stomach.

"Is there a shower on this plane?" I ask no one in particular.

"There are always showers on the planes we fly. And pajamas too! You should try the fluffy pajamas. They're the best," Rose says mid-bite.

"I'm going to go shower and try to find the fluffy pajamas then," I say.

I stand and head to the back of the plane. As I close the bathroom door, I hear Langston tell Rose he needs to make sure I find the pajamas and he needs to shower after me. I leave the door unlocked as I turn on the water in the small shower and strip my shirt just as Langston pushes in.

"Rose is smart, you know. If you keep showering at the same time as me, she's going to figure out that we are together."

"What's wrong with her knowing that we are together?"

I place my hand on his chest. "I'm just not ready yet."

He shakes his head. "I think we are way past time, Liesel.

You don't have a choice any longer. It's time whether you are ready or not. The kids deserve to know you. They deserve to know who you are, and we deserve to live happily ever after. Preferably with you spending lots and lots of time naked." He smirks.

I smile back, but a part of my smile is fake. I don't know how he thinks we can live happily ever after when we can't even say we love each other.

Instead of saying anything else, he just pushes us into the shower, clothes and all.

He catches my bottom lip and kisses me before I can say anything.

"I vow to make you feel good every chance I can, which means I owe you an orgasm."

I shake my head. "You made me come less than an hour ago. You don't need to make me co—"

I stop mid-word as his fingers press against my clit.

Holy cow.

A million tiny fireworks light up in my body when he touches me.

He flips me around until my back is pressed against his front while his hand continues to tease my sensitive nub. My pants are yanked to the floor, and the showerhead hits the front of my body, beginning to wash the blood away, along with the remnants of the other sacrifice I made.

Langston sweeps the hair off my neck as he kisses my bare skin. His fingers circle around my clit as more water bounces off my skin.

"I want—"

"No. This is about you—your pleasure. I'm tired of taking anything from you. You have to get at least double the amount of gratification as I do."

"But—"

There is no way I can finish that sentence, though.

All I can see are stars as I come once again. It's different than in the car. In the car, I was desperate. I needed to feel alive again—in control, connected to Langston.

This orgasm rips through my body, releasing all the feelings I've been hiding. All the feelings of pain I was holding back explode. Agony, despair, fear, loss—it hits me all at once.

"Let it all out, baby. I've got you."

It's at Langston's words that I realize I'm crying, trembling, shaking. I'm only standing because Langston is holding me up.

The water mixes with my tears and blood as it all goes down the drain. Everything we've been through—I let it all go. It's no longer my burden to bear.

We stay in the shower so long that we run out of water. At some point, we collapsed onto the floor, so I'm sitting in Langston's lap.

I look back. "You never took your clothes off."

"No, I was more concerned about making sure you were okay."

I kiss him softly. "I don't know what I would do without you."

"Me neither."

I am finally able to stand. I hold out my hand. He takes it, and I help him up. He's soaking wet and still covered in blood.

"I'm not sure the shower helped clean you that much," I say, looking him up and down.

He peels his shirt off. "Sure, it did."

I take a washcloth and do my best to clean off the rest of the dried blood from his body. He slips out of his pants, and I get a better view of the pain he went through with a large gash in his thigh.

I brush my hand over it. If I hadn't already cried out all the pain, I would start in again.

He takes my hand and kisses it. "We are all going to be okay now. I promise."

I smile at his empty promises. He doesn't mean them to be empty, but he can't promise me the world when the world doesn't belong to me.

"So, where are these fluffy pajamas?" I ask.

He laughs. "I think Rose means the fluffy white robes."

He grabs one on the hook behind me and drapes it over my shoulders.

I slip my arms through it and then wrap the sash around my waist. "Rose is right; these are fluffy."

Langston wraps the other robe around him.

He opens one of the drawers in the bathroom and pulls out two pairs of boxers for us both to slip on underneath our robes. Now we're decent enough to go back out with everyone on the plane.

"Ready?" he asks with his hand on the doorknob.

I nod.

He kisses me one more time, opens the door, and we walk back to the plane's main cabin.

Rose is talking animatedly to Enzo and Kai, who just nod along, encouraging her.

"Much better, now you don't look all icky anymore," Rose says as we sit on either side of her.

I yawn.

"I think it's time for us all to sleep," Langston says, giving Rose a stare that warns her from arguing with him.

She yawns. "Okay, fine."

"Is it okay if Liesel sleeps with us too?" he asks.

Rose nods. "She saved me. I don't want her to be afraid if she sleeps alone."

Langston motions for us all to stand, and he converts the

couch into a small bed. Kai gathers some blankets and pillows for us.

"We're going to sleep up front," Kai says, and then she and Enzo leave.

Langston climbs into the bed in his fluffy robe. Rose climbs in next. I'm slow to move, too busy watching the beautiful sight.

"Liesel, get in the bed. I'm cold, and your robe will keep me warm," Rose says.

I climb into bed and snuggle up next to Rose. Langston's arm wraps around us both. My eyes grow heavy, but I fight sleep as long as I can, wanting to memorize this incredible moment forever. I can't wait to have this moment with all of my children.

THE PLANE LANDS with Rose and Liesel snuggled up against me. We slept the entire flight, and it still doesn't seem like enough. I feel like I could sleep a month, and it wouldn't satisfy me. That's why we are all going to my private island—to rest, recover, and end our enemies once and for all.

Snuggling with my two girls was amazing, but my heart isn't full. It won't be until Atlas and Declan are both here.

We have a lot to figure out. *How do we introduce Liesel to the kids? What do we tell them about Phoenix? How do we ensure the Browns and the rest of our enemies don't come after us? What are we going to do about the treasure?*

None of that matters right now, though. In a few short hours, we are all going to be together. And once we are together, nothing will rip us apart again.

Kai walks into our section of the cabin, carrying a pile of clothes. "I found these for you guys to wear."

"Thanks," I say before waking Liesel with a kiss on the forehead. I can't bear to wake up Rose.

Liesel stirs and takes the clothes wordlessly back to the bathroom to change while Rose sleeps.

I put on the T-shirt and then slip into my pants while Rose continues to sleep. Carefully, I shift my arms under her body and then carry her off the plane to one of the waiting cars my staff drove over.

Rose murmurs something but stays asleep as I lay her in the backseat of the car. Liesel is right behind me. I motion for her to climb into the front seat as I jump into the driver's seat.

Enzo and Kai ride in another car with the staff behind us.

We don't speak as I drive us to my house. But I know we are both thinking about the last time we were here—me taking her, making her hike through the forest, threatening her life.

"I'm sorry," I say, knowing it's not enough.

"Me too," Liesel says back.

"You have nothing to be sorry for," I say.

She smiles thinly at me and then looks out the window, not responding.

As soon as we stop in front of the house, a switch flips in Rose, and she pops her head up.

"We came back here! This is my favorite home!" Rose says, throwing the door open and racing out.

"Her happiness is infectious," Liesel says.

"It is, but she knows how to use it to get what she wants," I say, raising my eyebrows as Rose throws open Liesel's door, grabs her hand, and drags her into the house, excited to show her around. She doesn't realize that Liesel has already been to the house before, back when I was a jackass, married to the wrong woman, and thought Liesel was the devil.

Kai and Enzo walk up behind me. "Our kids and Siren and Zeke's son are getting flown here as well. We want to be all together."

"Good," I say, gripping Enzo's shoulder. It's about time we were all together as a family.

Then I walk inside to look for my girls.

At first, I don't hear them, just the eery silence of a house that I haven't lived in for months, but then I hear Rose's giggling from upstairs followed by Liesel's laughter.

I decide to head to the kitchen to make coffee and breakfast, letting them have time to bond.

Rose is a good judge of character and outgoing, so it doesn't surprise me that she instantly took to Liesel. She knows Liesel is a good person instinctually, but Atlas isn't so trusting, and Declan is a mystery. We have no idea what he's been through or where he's been his whole life. Whatever has happened, we will figure out how to heal together.

Enzo walks into the kitchen as I start filling the coffee machine with grounds.

"Siren and Zeke's plane will be here in thirty minutes. The kid's plane about twenty minutes after that. And Beckett's plane will land in about an hour and a half."

"Good. After everyone is settled, we can all talk about what to do next."

Kai enters the room. "I have most of our fleet surrounding this island, protecting us. No one gets through unless we want them to."

"Thank you," I say.

She nods stiffly. "Phoenix is being held on one of the yachts just offshore. Just tell us what you want us to do with her."

I let out a long sigh. Deciding what to do with Phoenix is going to be difficult. Instead of thinking about it, I make coffee, eggs, bacon, toast. I mindlessly cook while people come in and out of the kitchen.

Rose, eventually drawn by the smell of bacon, brings Liesel down from playing tea party in her room.

I hand Liesel a cup of coffee, knowing she needs it to regain her energy after what we've been through. To my surprise, Liesel also makes herself a plate of eggs and bacon.

I smile, happy to see her finally eating something.

"Can I have some of your coffee?" Rose asks Liesel. I watch from the door as they sit out on the back deck, looking out at the ocean. Rose is an expert manipulator, and I want to see how Liesel handles her.

"Are you allowed to have coffee?" Liesel asks her.

"I am if an adult says I can," Rose bats her eyelashes.

Liesel tries to hide her laugh, but she can't. "You should ask your dad."

"But I don't want to run all the way inside," Rose whines.

"You can have some," I say as I walk over to them. Although I wish Liesel would feel like she can decide for herself what Rose can or can't do, she is her mother after all.

Liesel holds her cup up to Rose with a sly, knowing grin, but she doesn't say anything as she lets Rose take a drink. Rose, being Rose, takes a sip, doesn't like it, but won't say she doesn't like it because she wants to act like a grown-up.

"Do you like it?" Liesel asks.

"Dad doesn't make the best coffee. I like it better from Starbucks."

I frown. "When are you drinking coffee from Starbucks?"

She shrugs. "It tastes more chocolatey from Starbucks."

I laugh. "That's because I order you a hot chocolate from Starbucks, not coffee."

"Oh, well, I like that better."

I shake my head at her.

"So, do you live here now?" Rose asks Liesel.

Liesel looks to me for help, but I'm not going to help her.

"Would you like that?" Liesel asks her.

Rose pulls on the end of her shirt and decides to change the subject. "When is Atlas coming?"

I glance at my phone to check the time. "Any minute now."

"Good," she says, closing her eyes and letting the sun hit her face.

We relax, enjoying the sun and watching the road until two black SUVs roll up. We all jump up and run to the driveway as the cars come to a rolling stop.

Rose gets to the SUVs before Liesel or I do.

She throws open the back door and sticks her head in to find Atlas.

"Atlas!" I hear her happy cry as she wraps her arms around him.

"Okay, Rose, let him breathe," I say as I step up behind her.

She doesn't listen. She lifts him out of the car, still hugging onto him.

I shake my head, but I feel the same urge, so I wrap my arms tightly around them both. There was a time that holding them both in my arms made me feel whole, but not anymore.

Not without Liesel.

Not without Declan.

Right now, I feel the parts of me that are missing.

I don't know how to introduce Atlas to Liesel. He's more timid and cautious than Rose, and this is all a lot for Liesel.

"Liesel, come here," Rose says in a frustrated tone.

Liesel rushes over. "What's wrong?"

Rose lets Atlas go long enough to take his hand. "Atlas, this is Liesel. I know she has a funny name, but she saved my life, so she's one of us now."

Atlas falls into Liesel's arms, shocking the hell out of Rose and me. Liesel collapses her arms around him. They don't speak; they don't need to. Apparently, they already have a strong connection.

Finally, Atlas lets go of Liesel.

Rose's jaw has dropped to the floor. "How did you do that? Who are you?"

Liesel brushes Rose's cheek. "That's a question for another day."

Rose blinks rapidly and then takes Atlas' hand again. "Are you okay? Did they hurt you?"

"No, I'm not hurt. Uncle Zeke and Aunt Siren saved me. Are you hurt? I should have been there to protect you," Atlas says.

"No, I'm good. And that's okay; Liesel saved me," Rose says.

The two run off toward the house hand-in-hand.

We should get them some therapy and make sure they don't have lasting effects, but for now, they seem like they are going to be okay.

Zeke and Siren are both standing to the side of one of the SUVs. Liesel and I walk over to them.

"Thank you," we both say at the same time. We both hug each of them.

"Are you okay? We can never repay you for what you did," Liesel says.

Siren opens her mouth but doesn't speak.

Zeke is staring at Siren like he's trying to read her thoughts.

They both look like we do—exhausted, worn down, bruised, and cut up. It wouldn't surprise me if they are slow to answer or process what we are saying, but they aren't talking at all. Something's wrong.

I walk up to Siren, my eyes searching for an answer. I touch her arm. We've always shared a connection that I don't understand.

Somehow all three of our families are connected through a bond different than the ones we have with our spouses. My connection is with Siren. Zeke has a connection with Kai. Liesel has a connection with Enzo. It's a strange circle, but it's our family.

When I touch her, I know something is wrong. My eyes search hers; I can feel loss inside of her.

"Siren lost her voice. I lost my hearing," Zeke says.

Siren nods, once again, not speaking.

I grab her head and pull her tightly to my body, needing to comfort her in some way. Once I've tried to take away some of her pain, I look to Zeke.

"Explain," I say as slowly as I can, mouthing my word to him.

He knows what I'm asking, though, even without looking.

"The game. In order to win and save Atlas, we both had to play a sacrifice card. The card made us sacrifice something. They poured liquid in my ears and Siren's throat, burning my eardrums and her vocal cords. We think the damage is temporary. My ears are already starting to ring, but we should have a doctor see if there is anything they can do to speed the healing up," Zeke says. His voice is shaky and tentative as he speaks since he can't hear himself talk.

"You shouldn't have given up your voice or your hearing," I say, completely speechless at the sacrifice they were both willing to make.

Siren tries to speak, but I can see how much pain stabs into her throat when she tries. She frowns and shakes her hand at Zeke, who pulls out a pen and paper from his pocket and hands it to her.

She starts scribbling furiously and then holds it up to me. Liesel looks at it over my shoulder as well.

· · ·

It was our choice. We wanted to make the sacrifice to save Atlas. He's like a son to us. It was just my voice, just Zeke's hearing. Both can heal, and even if they don't, it will still have been worth it. Saving Atlas' life was worth it.

She's scribbled three lines under the last sentence.

"I'm going to find a way to heal you," I look at Siren, then Zeke. "Both of you."

Siren rolls her eyes and huffs.

"I understand that it's not about that. Thank you. You did your part though, let me do mine," I say, hugging Siren again.

I'm so consumed by my concern for Siren and Zeke that it takes me a minute to realize what this means. To win his game, Beckett also had to sacrifice something in order to save Declan. *What did he have to sacrifice?*

And then my heart drops even further as I look at Liesel; she's watching me carefully. She said she won her game to ensure they wouldn't have a reason to get Rose back.

What did she sacrifice?

18

LIESEL

LANGSTON FIGURED IT OUT. He knows that I sacrificed some-thing; he just doesn't know what.

Langston looks at me as Zeke rests his arm around Siren's shoulders, and they start walking together toward the house.

I freeze. I'm not ready for this conversation. I'm tired of lying to Langston, but I'm not ready to tell him the truth yet either.

He walks toward me, presumably to ask me what I sacri-ficed. Instead, he kisses me tenderly on the lips.

The kiss tells me everything I need to know. He's here when I'm ready to tell him. I take his hand and let him lead me back inside the house.

"I'm headed back to the airport to get the kids," Enzo says.

We are so close to all being safe, so close.

"I need to make a phone call," Langston says, kissing my hand before stepping away.

I notice Rose and Atlas watching me closely from the

119

living room. They both have their suspicions about me, about this whole situation. They deserve answers, but we need to wait until everyone is here before we talk. There is no use in having this conversation twice.

So instead, I walk into the kitchen, open the freezer and pull out a pint of ice cream. I grab three spoons and walk over to where the kids are sitting on the couch and hand them each a spoon.

"More ice cream?" Rose asks incredulously.

"Atlas didn't get any the last time."

We sit together and eat ice cream. They deserve to know who I am. They deserve the whole truth. Honestly, I'd just be fine if I was the ice cream lady to them.

———

Enzo returns with his twins and Cayden, Zeke and Siren's baby.

The twins run to Kai, and Enzo joins them.

Siren scoops up Cayden, who has just started walking. She goes to speak to him, then stops herself when she realizes that she can't. She catches me watching her and smiles before kissing Cayden all over his face, which makes him laugh hysterically.

"We missed you, little man," Zeke says, grabbing him up and swinging him around, making him laugh more. Zeke smiles brightly at him, not showing any outward sign at all that he's upset he can't hear his child's laughter.

But it breaks my heart.

It shouldn't be this way. Their family shouldn't pay because of something my father did.

"We're going to fix it," Langston says, coming up next to me.

I look at him.

"I called some doctors that specialize in hearing and vocal cords. They will be out here tomorrow. We are going to get them fixed."

I nod, hopeful but unsure if it's as easy as that.

We hear another car pull up; Langston and I exchange worried glances.

The last car is here, early.

Beckett.

Declan.

"Kai, watch Atlas and Rose, please," Langston shouts as he tries to catch up with me. I'm already running outside.

We don't know the tortured state Beckett could be in. He already went through so much when he lost his arm. I can't imagine what else he could have lost.

More importantly, I need to see Declan with my own two eyes. I need to know that he's alive and that he's here—safe.

Beckett throws open the passenger door. He walks over slow and steady to us. He's covered in blood. His shirt and pants are ripped like he was just attacked by a mountain lion. And his hand has a shirt wrapped around it.

But none of that is what has me concerned. My heart is beating a thousand miles a second because of the look in his eyes—complete sorrow.

"I'm so sorry," Beckett says.

"You lost?" Langston snaps a little too harshly.

I put my hand on Langston's shoulder and shake my head, trying to remind Langston that even if he did lose, it's not Beckett's fault. He did the best he could.

But I don't think that's what Beckett is saying.

It's clear he fought.

He played the game and did the dares, based on the injuries he has. He played the sacrifice card, and from the looks of it, he sacrificed his other hand. He already told us that he won.

"Corbin didn't give you Declan even after you won, did he?" I ask.

"He gave me a child, but that child wasn't Declan. I'm sorry."

"How did you know he wasn't Declan?" Langston asks.

"I know Rose and Atlas. I know their features, their mannerisms, their size. This child was bigger, older. His skin was tanner. He didn't share any of Rose, Atlas, or Liesel's features. I have some of his hair if you want to run a DNA test, but the child isn't yours, Liesel."

A tear starts to roll, but I wipe it away quickly.

"Where is the child?" Langston asks, still not convinced.

"He's with his parents. I did a quick search of the missing child reports. There was one from a few months ago that matched his description. He has a sister with reddish-brown hair that matches his."

Langston looks at me like he needs my assurance.

I sit down, right in the middle of the driveway. I don't have the energy to stand anymore. I just need a minute to process all of this.

"We should run the DNA test just to confirm, but it doesn't sound like that child is mine," I say.

"Then, where is Declan?" Langston asks.

Dead?

Missing?

With Corbin?

I don't know the answer, but we have to find out. Until I know for sure where Declan is, I have to keep searching, hunting. I'm the huntress, after all, and I won't give up. Corbin and Maxwell are still out there. They could still have him.

Langston sits down next to me on one side. Beckett slumps down on the other.

Seeing his bandaged hand breaks me. "Oh my god, you went through all that pain for nothing. You lost your other hand for nothing."

Beckett shakes his head. "It wasn't for nothing. I saved that kid. I don't regret it." He unwraps his hand, revealing boils and burns all over his skin. "And I didn't lose my hand, just my sense of touch and attractiveness until this heals."

Langston whips out his phone. "I'm going to call for a doctor to look at those ASAP. I already have specialists flying out tomorrow for Siren and Zeke."

He stands and walks a short distance away to make the call.

"Siren and Zeke are okay?" Beckett asks.

"Yes, Siren sacrificed her voice; Zeke, his hearing."

"And the kids?"

"Rose and Atlas are safe and sound. They aren't injured in any way we can see. I think Langston has a pediatrician and psychologist coming out to check on them just to be sure, but they seem perfectly fine. When I left them, they were eating a tub of ice cream."

He smiles at that.

"Thank you, Beckett. You have no idea how much your sacrifice means to me, even if it didn't turn out the way we planned."

"It was the right thing to do—no regrets."

We both turn and look out at the ocean. The sun is already beginning to set. Where did the time go?

"What happens now?" Beckett asks.

Langston returns, standing over my shoulder.

I turn to answer Beckett. "First, we talk to the kids. We tell them the truth or as much of the truth as they can handle. Then we make a plan to find Declan and protect all of us from Corbin, Maxwell, and Phoenix."

Langston lowers his hand to me. I reluctantly take it.

I'm not sure I'm doing what's best for Rose and Atlas by telling them the truth. A large part of me still feels like I should hide the truth from them to protect them, but the other part wants to love them openly.

That part can't be silenced any longer.

19

LANGSTON

"THEY ARE GOING to love you. There is nothing you should be nervous about," I tell Liesel as we walk back into the house, Beckett trailing behind.

I can tell she's nervous, her hands are shaking at her sides, and she doesn't respond.

"Or we can go with the whole hate me thing we got going on. They'll think that's a hoot," I joke.

I tilt my head, hoping she'll crack a smile—she doesn't. She's a woman on a mission, and I have no choice but to go along with it and hope she's ready to tell the truth. *Maybe after she tells the kids the truth, she can start talking to me?*

We head back inside, and Liesel freezes. I'm guessing she's having second thoughts, but I'm not going to let her think too hard about this. She needs to tell the kids who she is. It's the only way we can be a family again.

"Rose, Atlas, you want to go for a walk on the beach with Liesel and me?"

"Yes!" Rose says immediately.

Atlas nods, and they both pop off the couch.

Beckett walks in behind us, and Kai runs to him,

engulfing him in a hug. They all have a lot to talk about, so I take Liesel's hand and lead her out the back deck, then down the stairs toward the beach. Rose and Atlas chase after us.

As we get closer to the beach, I find a quiet spot and sit down. Liesel doesn't sit immediately, so I tug on her hand until she takes the hint and sits.

"Are we building sandcastles?" Rose asks.

I shake my head. "Maybe later. We both wanted to talk to you about something first. Liesel is…"

Jesus, it's harder to tell my kids their whole world has changed than I realized. And if I tell them Liesel is their birth mom, do I have to tell Rose that I'm not her biological father?

I rub my neck, unsure of what to do next when Liesel speaks.

"I'm your birth mother."

Both Rose and Atlas snap their head to Liesel.

"Whose? Mine or Atlas'?" Rose asks, staring at Liesel in awe.

"Both. See, once upon a time, I was a young woman, and I got pregnant with three special children."

"Three?" Atlas blinks.

"Yes, three. I was young and scared, but I loved my three babies more than anything in the world. Those babies were you, Rose." She smiles at Rose. "And you, Atlas." She turns her smile to Atlas. "And another baby named Declan."

Neither of the kids ask questions anymore. They are entranced with Liesel's story.

"The day came that you three were finally ready to leave my belly. I got sick and fell asleep when you were born. Someone took you three away before I got a chance to see you or hold you. You were split up and given to different people to live with.

"Rose, you were given to your mother, Phoenix, and your father, Langston. Atlas—eventually, Phoenix and Langston found you. They didn't know that you and Rose were biological brother and sister at the time, but they knew you belonged to this family all the same."

He smiles up at her.

"Now, we are looking for your brother, Declan, to complete the family."

"We really have another brother?" Atlas asks.

Liesel nods.

She reaches forward and takes both of their hands. "What you need to know, though, is that even though I wasn't around, I still loved you and tried my best to protect you all your lives. Langston, your father, is your father in every way that matters. Phoenix—" She takes a deep breath.

"Phoenix is still your mother. She loves you desperately, and she's helping us find your brother. We all love you. Your mom, dad, me, and all your aunts, uncles, and cousins inside. We all love you."

I'm not sure about telling them that Phoenix is still their mother and loves them, but everything else is spot on.

"Do you have any questions for your father or me?"

"Can we call you Mom?" Rose asks.

Liesel smiles. "You can call me whatever you want."

"What do we call Mom, though?" Atlas asks, confused.

"You can call your other mom, Mom, too. You can have two moms."

"I like that idea," Atlas says.

"Are you two dating?" Rose asks, looking from Liesel to me.

"That's a complicated question, but yes, we are," Liesel replies.

"What about our other mom? Do you not love her anymore, Dad? Where is she?" Rose asks.

"She's looking for Declan, but I have a feeling she'll be

back soon," Liesel says, stepping in before I can answer, forcing me to follow her lead.

"I love both of your moms very much in very different ways. We still have a lot to figure out as a family, but we are all a family. All of us in our own complicated way, okay?" I say.

All three pairs of lips smile and nod at me while I get a queasy feeling in my stomach. I trust Liesel with my life; I just hope she knows what she's doing.

2 0

LIESEL

WE PUT ALL the kids to bed, and then it's just the adults sitting in the living room.

Kai sits on the floor, leaning against Enzo's knees. Siren and Zeke sit snuggled together, a large legal pad and pen lying on their lap so Siren can communicate.

Beckett sits in a single chair with his hand in a new bandage. He has a smoothie with a straw, so he can lean over to get some calories until a doctor looks at his hand.

Langston and I sit on a loveseat with Langston's arm around my shoulders, just as much a couple as the rest of them. I twirl my ring around my finger. We talked to the kids. They know almost everything and took it surprisingly well, even though it's ridiculously complicated. Now we all have to decide what we do next.

There would have been a time when I thought it was just my and Langston's decision. I thought everyone in the room betrayed us, but now that everyone has sacrificed so much, I know differently. We are a family, no matter what happens.

"So, what do we do next?" Kai asks, starting the conversation.

129

All eyes fall on us.

"We talk to Phoenix," I say immediately, even though I know the whole room will disagree with me. There is no immediate outrage, at least not from anyone except Langston, who looks at me like I'm off my rocker.

Siren jots down what I said, so Zeke is up to speed. I get no protest from them either. I do need to remember to pause after I speak, so they can get caught up.

"For now, we have to assume Corbin and Maxwell have Declan. Phoenix is likely to confirm or deny it, so let's start there," I say.

There's some nodding from the room.

"Phoenix won't tell us the truth. We will gain nothing from talking to her," Langston says, removing his arm from behind me.

I miss the loss immediately.

"She told us the truth about the clubs."

"No, if she did, then we would already have Declan."

"We have Rose and Atlas because of the information she gave us. And they didn't hurt the kids. If she truly wanted to hurt us, then they would have hurt them—they didn't. They just want more from us. We need to talk to her."

"Or we could attack Corbin and Maxwell. Kill them and their team, extract Declan ourselves, if they even have him."

"And what would you do with Phoenix?"

"She doesn't deserve to live after what she's done," Langston says.

I sigh. He's just being a protective father. He feels betrayed by her. But every person in this room has hurt and betrayed people, oftentimes betraying others in this room. We're all human, and we have all fucked up when we were hurting or trying to protect others. Everyone deserves a second chance.

"It's no longer just up to us to decide, so let's put it to a vote. Should our next step be talking to Phoenix or not?" I ask the room.

Langston stares them down, trying to persuade them to his side. It wouldn't shock me if they took his side, simply because they are closer to him than they are to me.

"Enzo?" Langston asks.

"I don't trust Phoenix, so no, I don't think you should talk to her. I agree with Langston—we should attack Corbin and Maxwell, then find Declan once we've destroyed them," Enzo says.

Kai looks at me with sympathy in her eyes and says, "I agree with Enzo."

That's two for Langston and none for me. It's not looking good.

We all turn our attention to Siren and Zeke. Siren is writing furiously on the paper, and Zeke is studying every word closely. He looks at Siren, who nods at him.

"Siren agrees with Liesel. We should get every bit of information we can from Phoenix. And for the kids' sake, she deserves a second chance," Zeke speaks.

That makes it two to one, but Zeke and Beckett will take Langston's side.

Zeke thinks for a moment and then speaks. "I also agree with Liesel."

I blink rapidly, not sure I heard him correctly. Two to two.

Everyone's attention turns to Beckett.

"You're the deciding vote, Beckett," Langston says.

Beckett stares at his injured hand. He's lost the most. Sure, Siren lost her voice and Zeke his hearing, but they can rely on each other to make up for the losses.

And I lost...

But Beckett has no one to help him. He was already at a

disadvantage, and now that his other hand is injured, he's going to struggle without a lot of help.

"We have to do what gives us the best chance to get Declan back. Talk to Phoenix, find out what she knows. Then, you can decide what the best course of action is to get Declan back."

Langston stands in a huff. I think he's going to storm out, frustrated with the group's decision. He holds his hand out to me instead.

Carefully, I place my hand in his.

"Fine, let's get this over with," Langston says.

LANGSTON

I GOT OUTVOTED.

That's why I'm currently climbing on board a yacht instead of planning a tactical mission to take out Corbin and everyone who works for him. Being on the ocean like this used to be my sanctuary, but now it's my nightmare. Anywhere my kids aren't is my nightmare.

Liesel stands next to me on the top deck as we ask one of the employees where they're keeping Phoenix. He gives us her room number and the code to get in before walking away to continue his duties.

We head downstairs to her room. My hand hovers over the security keypad outside her room.

"You sure?" I ask Liesel.

She nods. "Phoenix is not a bad person. She's done some horrible things because she's hurting, and she doesn't know how to deal with the pain. She'll help us."

I'm not sure if I agree with her, but I enter the code and open the door. I step inside first; I'll do anything I can to protect Liesel.

Phoenix is sitting on the bed, staring out a window,

looking out at the ocean. She doesn't glance over at us as we enter.

"So, you failed and are begging me to convince my brothers to give you your kids back, huh?" Phoenix asks.

I'm about to yell at her, attack her, squeeze her until she pays for everything she's put us through.

"No, that's not why we are here," Liesel says, stepping out from behind me.

Phoenix snaps her head to Liesel.

I grab Liesel's hand, trying to keep her back. Phoenix is going to try to attack her.

Liesel shakes me off. She walks over and sits on the foot of the bed staring at Phoenix.

"We won the games," Liesel says.

"You got the kids back?" Phoenix asks.

"We got Rose and Atlas back," Liesel says.

Phoenix exhales, her shoulders visibly relaxing, acting relieved. But then she looks Liesel in the eyes with concern. "You sacrificed? All of you?"

"We did," she says quietly.

Phoenix nods.

"We did our part. We felt the pain. We hurt. We won, but we only got Rose and Atlas back. We didn't get Declan. Corbin gave Beckett another kid, not Declan," Liesel says.

Phoenix looks down as she picks her nails.

"Phoenix? Does Corbin even have Declan?"

She nods.

"How do we get him back?"

"I'm sorry," Phoenix says, looking from Liesel to me. "Truly, I am. I never wanted the kids to suffer. I only wanted to hurt you."

"Will Corbin hurt Declan?" I ask. If he would, I'm not waiting. I'll fight Corbin to the death right now. I'm not going to wait for whatever games.

"No, he just doesn't think you all have suffered enough."

"What do you think?" Liesel asks.

Phoenix exchanges a glance with Liesel. "I think once you finish the games, you'll have paid me back for the pain your father caused me."

"So, how do we finish the game?" I ask.

"You get the treasure. You give it to Corbin. You set me free, and you promise to never attack my family again."

That's not something I can promise.

"Can I ask for something?" Phoenix asks.

"No," I say, at the same time Liesel says, "Yes."

"I'd like to say goodbye to the kids. I know you don't think I deserve it, but I want to explain to them why they won't be seeing me anymore when the time comes," Phoenix says.

"No," I say, walking out the door. I'm done with her. I don't trust her. She's manipulative and did the one thing I view as unforgivable—hurt my children.

I'm nearly out the door before I hear Liesel say, "He'll come around. He's just hurt. We'll figure something out when it comes to the kids."

I head up to the top deck of the yacht and lean over the edge of the railing, looking out as the moon rises over the ocean.

Liesel stands next to me.

"Are you upset with me?" she asks.

I inhale a deep breath. "No, I can't be upset with you, even when we disagree—not anymore."

"You can be mad at me and still care for me. I'm sure you get mad at the kids sometimes, but that doesn't mean you don't love them."

I shake my head. "I'm not upset with you. I just disagree with you. And I'm upset with myself that you don't trust me enough to tell me what you sacrificed so I can help you heal."

She sighs as she leans further over the edge of the railing.

"What if I told you the sacrifice I made didn't matter because I already lost that part of me years ago? The reason I don't want to tell you is that nothing has changed. I don't want you to think I was suffering and you weren't there to stop it when it's not true."

I frown. "I'd say that whatever you went through, no matter how small, I want to know. I need to protect you. I need—"

"No, you don't. Sometimes, it's better if you don't know."

We are both silent a moment.

"What do we have to do to get the next clue to the treasure?" she asks.

"You really think finding the treasure, and playing their games, is the best way to get Declan back?"

"Yes, I do," she says.

God, help us.

"What is it? What aren't you telling me?" Liesel asks.

Fucking everything.

"Nothing—it's nothing."

She folds her arms and faces me. "Tell me the truth, killer."

"You go first."

She frowns.

"Fine, we both keep our secrets. If it means we're protecting each other, then I agree we shouldn't tell each other."

"Fine."

"Fine."

"Now what?"

Now, I make you admit you love me instead of hating me while trying to keep my own feelings hidden so I don't destroy us all.

How do I make her fall in love with me?

Romance.

I've tried it before and failed, but I don't know what else to try. Maybe a day away from all of this will make her admit her feelings. One day where we aren't thinking about the kids or how to protect our family and friends.

"One day," I say.

"What?"

"Give me one day where you don't ask any questions. We forget about the past, our future, the kids, the danger—everything. Give me one day where it's just us. Can you do that?"

She bites her lip, and I expect her to say I'm crazy, but then she says, "Yes."

I KNOW SOMETHING IS UP. There is a reason Langston wants to spend a day together. A day where I just go along with whatever he has planned and not ask any questions. A day where I forget that I still have a child in danger and that my other two children are on an island, still in danger as long I keep waiting to finish this ridiculous treasure quest.

But I trust Langston.

I trust him too much.

So when he calls his team to bring us his sailboat, I climb on, no questions asked.

We are as safe as humanly possible. Kai has her entire team out on boats surrounding and protecting us, but it still feels strange to be on a boat by ourselves.

I sit on the side of the boat as I watch Langston work, pulling on ropes and getting the sail into the position he wants. At one point, he loses his shirt, giving me an exquisite view of his rippling muscles.

Finally, he must be satisfied with the work he's done on the sail. He reaches into a cooler and pulls out a bottle of champagne and a couple of flutes.

"Come here," he says, sitting and patting the spot in front of his lap.

My stomach does a little flip as I sit in his lap. If he were truly mine, then sitting between his legs under the stars while we sip champagne would be the most romantic thing in the world. Despite the fact that we are legally married, despite the fact that we care deeply for each other, have said that we belong to each other, it's not true.

He's not mine.

I repeat those words to myself as I lean back against his bare chest.

He hands me a glass of champagne, which I take, even though I don't want any alcohol tonight. I have a feeling I'll be replaying this night forever in my head, and I don't want to forget a single detail.

His arms wrap around my stomach, pulling me tighter against his chest until we can both look up at the stars.

Then Langston starts softly singing John Legend's 'All of Me.' My heart stops beating as he sings the first verse, wondering what's going on in my mind. Next, my breathing stops as he nears the chorus. I wait to hear the words I've been dying to hear from him since I was seventeen, maybe even longer.

"...*hates* all of you," he sings, changing the lyrics.

I chuckle. It's what the moment needs, but god, does it sting to not hear him sing the one word that's missing from my life.

But if he were to say he loves me, it will end up killing him. It's for the best.

Tell that to my lovesick heart.

He continues to sing the rest of the song, and every time he says 'hate' instead of 'love,' I wince. He must notice, but he doesn't say anything.

Finally, when my heart can't take anymore, I get up from

his lap and walk to the other end of the boat. Maybe I should have drunk some of that champagne after all?

"You okay?" Langston asks.

I nod, not trusting my voice.

His hand slides up and down my back. "You're tense. How about a soak in the tub and massage?"

I nod again.

I feel his breath on my neck; I hiss because he feels so good without even touching me. I can't fight giving him my heart anymore. It's his—it's always been his. Now to decide if it's fair to tell him or not.

He walks away from me, removing the cover of the hot tub. He presses a button to turn it on, and bubbles come to life.

I smile. Only Langston would have a sailboat with a hot tub on the top deck.

Silently, he walks back to me. We haven't spoken much since he sang his song. He grabs the hem of my shirt and pulls it up and over my body. Then he moves to my pants, taking his time sliding them down my body until I'm in nothing but boxers from the plane.

He sucks in a breath as his eyes rake over my bare chest. He hooks his fingers into the waistband and pushes them down too.

"Are you going undress me, or do I have to do that too?" he asks with a smirk.

"You seem to be doing a pretty good job yourself."

His grin turns vicious. He shoves his pants and boxers down in one push before yanking us backward into the hot tub.

The water engulfs us, warmth soothing my aching muscles, but his body against mine is cruel. I want him forever, instead of just this one fairytale of a day.

We surface, and I'm once again sitting on Langston's lap.

He starts working my shoulders, and I melt. I try to push out my fears and do what Langston said—just enjoy tonight. His touch helps. I can't help but relax.

"Where should we go on our honeymoon?" Langston asks suddenly.

I turn my head to look at him. "What honeymoon?"

"The honeymoon we are going to go on after we get Declan."

"But—"

Langston kisses my lips, shutting me up. "Where?"

When I still don't speak, Langston says, "Humor me. Do you want to go somewhere warm? Another beach? The mountains?"

When I don't answer, he continues throwing out ideas. "Paris? The Maldives? Sydney? San Diego? St. Lucia?"

"Stop."

"What? I need to imagine a life after this—a month-long vacation that's just the two of us. I love our kids, but I want to do very dirty things to your body to make up for lost time, and I can't do that with them around. We'll make it up to them with a trip to Disney World or something afterward. And they'll have fun playing with Kai and Enzo's twins."

I scoot off his lap, wanting to look him in the eye when we talk.

"Does it bother you that our kids aren't biologically yours?" I know it doesn't, but it heals my heart to hear him talk about the kids, to know he will always be their father, no matter what else happens.

"No, it doesn't bother me. They're mine," he growls.

I smile.

"Even if their father wasn't a dead motherfucker, they would still belong to me."

Then another thought pops into my head that I can't dismiss; I have to know its answer. "I know you already think of Atlas and Rose as your kids and that you will feel the same way about Declan, but…"

"But what?"

"Do you want biological kids? Kids that look like you, share your mannerisms, your blood?"

"Rose already looks like me with her blonde hair and adventurous spirit. And Atlas mimics every behavior of mine that he can. The other day I caught him trying to use my razor to shave his face," he chuckles at the memory.

His laughter stops when he sees how serious I am. I need to know the truth.

His eyes drop to my stomach beneath the bubbles. He still thinks there is a chance I'm pregnant, that I can be the one to provide him with a biological child.

I should tell him the truth, but I can't—not yet. It could ruin his whole world, and not when there is still a tiny fraction of a chance that—

"No, I don't need a biological child. I have Rose, Atlas, Declan. I never thought I'd make a good father with the example I had as a father."

"Langston, you're a good father."

"I know. I'm not perfect, but I do my best, and our kids know I love them. Being loved by them, having you in my life, it's more than I could have ever imagined. I don't need a kid that shares my blood to make me happy, but if one comes along, I'll love them too."

Can't. Feel. My. Heart.

"Is something wrong?" Langston asks.

I shake my head.

He snickers knowingly. "Something you want to tell me?"

I shake more furiously.

He laughs and relaxes his arms over the edge of the hot tub, seemingly at ease with wherever this conversation is going.

"I always knew we'd end up married," he says.

"You did?"

"Of course. We both fought it because we are both so independent and stubborn, and we believed the lies. But I always knew you were it for me, huntress." I can't tell if he's glad that I'm the person for him or tormented that we are stuck together.

He notices my change. "Tell me something I don't know about you. Tell me a wish, a dream."

I run my tongue over the front of my teeth. There is a wicked gleam in my eyes. I don't have a wish or a dream for some far-off future other than ensuring that our kids are safe. I can't think or plan for our future. That's not something I want to imagine. It doesn't warm my heart to plan a honeymoon or pretend that our marriage can survive what's coming.

"I've never had sex in a hot tub under the stars," I say.

"Really? I thought everyone had," he teases.

I shake my head slowly, keeping my lust-filled eyes on him.

I'm tired of talking.

He's obviously trying for a romantic night, but I'm tired of it. I want dirty, filthy sex. That's the only thing that can get me out of my head right now.

I inch toward him; his arms stay on the edge of the tub. His eyes are already attacking me, roaming over every part of my body he intends to kiss, lick, tease. A rush of excitement spreads between my legs at the look.

I inch forward until I'm as close as I can get without touching him. Still, he doesn't try and touch me. When I glance at his hands, I see his knuckles are turning white. He's gripping onto the side of the tub to control himself.

"What are you doing?" I giggle at his ridiculousness.

"Trying to take my time so I can memorize every face

you make. How you sound when you breathe versus when I'm touching you. How you feel."

"You can't know how I feel if you don't touch me."

"If I touch you, I'm going to get caught up in fucking you and miss the glow you have, the fire in your eyes."

"What's wrong with getting lost in me?"

"Nothing—I just want to take my time with you."

I straddle his lap as I hold onto the tub on either side of his shoulders and let my body sink down on top of him.

"We only have one night. You don't get to take your time with me."

He frowns, but my comment finally makes him touch me. He grabs my hips as his pelvis tilts his hard length between my legs. He tilts his head forward, taking my bottom lip into his mouth. His growl rattles through our bodies.

"We are pretending the outside world doesn't exist for one night, but you are mine forever," he promises.

He lifts me up and then drives me down onto his cock, claiming me in one stroke.

"So much for going slow," I tease.

He responds by driving into me harder, shutting me up until I can no longer speak.

My body responds to his every thrust. My lips kiss his over and over. Our tongues collide and slide over each other.

Langston wants to take this slow to ensure we remember every second. I'd prefer to spend the night fucking over and over again until my body and brain can't forget how Langston feels inside my body.

"I belong in your body," Langston says.

"Yo—" I can't get any words out. He's fucking me so hard; he's rattling my brain cells. Shocks of emotions pulse through my body.

I don't know how he does this. I love sex; I've had plenty of good partners over the years. But with Langston, it's not about where we are, the mood, the scenery, or the position. Just being with him—kissing, licking, fucking, any of it—takes me to a different place. My body is overcome with some emotion I haven't felt before. I don't care if I come or how good it feels, as long as Langston and I are connecting.

"Come, baby," Langston growls.

He can sense how close I am. That growl thing he does, low and vibrating through my whole body, is all I need to come. I explode, and my eyes are seeing shooting stars in the sky above me. I still can't form coherent syllables, let alone words.

Langston is kissing my swollen lips slowly before he scoops me into his arms. "I hate you so much, Liesel. I hate you so much."

23

LANGSTON

THE SUN WAKES me as it begins to rise over the ocean. We slept on the top of the sailboat with a comforter snuggled around us. Liesel is still asleep on my shoulder.

I don't want to move her, but I failed last night. Liesel didn't admit she loves me. I'm going to have to try something different. We fucked three times last night. Each time was rough and frantic. It was all either of us could manage, but slow, romantic lovemaking is what this task needs; not feral, animalistic fucking.

I inch myself out from under Liesel. She continues to snore as I stand up. Then I run to the small kitchenette to make coffee and omelets.

After whipping up a quick breakfast, I return with a tray of food and coffee to where Liesel is still sleeping. I don't want to wake her; she looks so peaceful, and in our life, you sleep as much as you can. But every second we fail to get the treasure is another second our son is in danger, so this can't wait.

I slip under the covers next to Liesel, and then I hold one of the cups underneath Liesel's nose as I kiss her cheek.

"Good morning."

"Mmmh," she moans but doesn't open her eyes. "Am I dreaming, or is that coffee?"

"It's coffee."

Her eyes snap open, and she smiles at me with flushed cheeks.

I frown. There's a chill in the air; she shouldn't feel warm.

I brush my hand over her forehead—she does feel warm.

Her lips lean up to kiss mine, and I forget about her feeling warm.

"Sit up," I tell her.

She moves into the crook of my arm and leans against my shoulder. I hand her the cup of coffee and then move the tray across our laps so she can eat her omelet.

"Wow, I've never had breakfast in bed, but I'm not sure I can call a comforter on the deck of a boat a bed," she says.

"Is that a thank you?"

She grins. "Thank you."

"You're welcome."

We both drink our coffees and pick at our omelets. Liesel doesn't eat enough, but I'm not going to try to get her to change her eating habits now. She sets her almost empty coffee mug down on the tray.

"Why are we really here? I know you are doing this, so when you do the fucked up thing the task requires, I'll have some good memories to pair with it. But we are running out of time. Can we get to the hard part now?" Liesel says.

She's right; that's what this whole night and morning have been about. As much as I enjoy sitting here eating breakfast with her, it's not going to get her to admit she loves me. Hopefully, it is giving her warm and fuzzy feelings that might help her get there faster.

I set the tray to the side wordlessly. Yes, this is all about the stupid treasure, but I'm not treating her sweetly because

I plan on hurting her. It's the opposite. I want her to love me as I love her.

I grab her neck and lay her back down as my body moves over her. She's naked underneath the comforter, as am I. The feeling of our naked bodies touching overwhelms my senses, and I'm immediately hard again.

"What are you doing?" she asks, her bottom lip trembling just slightly.

Leaning down, I close my eyes and kiss that lip tenderly.

She gasps at the impact.

My intention is to worship every inch of her body. I want to make her know how much I love each part of her and that she's safe with me. I'll love her forever, no matter what happens. I want to flood her with feelings so that the words just fall out of her.

She can't take it back because once she speaks the truth, she's not going to be able to stop speaking or feeling it. I'm guessing that's why she hasn't spoken the words so far. She doesn't want to love me. She wants to go back to her independent life by herself and get visitation of the kids or some shit like that. She's scared; everyone she has ever loved has hurt her, left her, or been taken away from her.

She needs to know that I won't hurt her.

I won't leave her.

And I won't be taken from her.

I start at her forehead. I leave a kiss there and then move to each of her cheeks.

"Your eyes have captivated me since we were five, and we hunted a spider together," I say.

She smiles, her face heating.

My lips find the spot behind her ear that causes her breath to speed. Then I move to her earlobes, my tongue flicking the lobe until she gasps.

"I want to worship your entire body forever. Will you let me?"

"Mmmh," she moans.

I grin. "I'll take that as a yes."

I kiss her lips gently, trying not to get carried away and fuck her too fast.

"Every time I kiss you, your lips hold me captive. I get swept away in your delicious lips. Your taste. Your moans. It's everything I've ever dreamed of."

I kiss down her neck until I'm licking down her clavicle. She shifts underneath me as I move closer to the upper curve of her breast.

"And your curves drive me wild, Liesel."

I find her first nipple with my teeth, teasing it gently as I swirl my tongue along the tip. When I move to the second, she arches her back and sinks her hand into my hair, becoming even more breathless.

"You still with me?" I smile around her other nipple. I want her to feel amazing, but I also need her able to talk. It's a fine balance.

She groans.

"I'm going to need an actual answer, or I might have to stop." I flick her nipple with my tongue.

"Fuck," she curses.

"That's better, baby."

I continue my way down her body, kissing over her stomach. I take my time here, still not convinced she's not pregnant. Her questions from earlier about wanting a biological child of my own pop into my head. My hopes of her being pregnant have nothing to do with my own feelings. Although, it does make me possessive as hell to think I put a baby in her belly. I hope she's pregnant because she missed out on so much with the kids' early days. She should get to experience that.

She notices that I spend extra time on her belly.

"I hate you," she says, once again avoiding saying the real words. I almost regret starting the hate you line.

We are getting close, baby. Just say the actual words.

"You're the most incredible mother. This whole time you've been protecting them, loving them. Just fucking amazing."

I spread her legs, deciding she's earned my attention on her most sensitive area—the part she's been trying to push me toward with her hand in my hair and the arch of her back.

I lick up her slit.

"Jesus, Langston."

There's my girl.

I hold her legs apart as I find her clit with my tongue and swirl around it. She bends her knees, and her legs fall further open, giving me better access. My tongue pushes inside her, finding her soaking before I lick her clit again and again.

"You taste so sweet. And yet, you are the strongest woman I know."

I slide two fingers inside her, intensifying her pleasure before I make her come. I barely push inside her before I feel her clenching around me. Her nails dig into my skull as she grips my hair. She moans and screams my name, but nothing for her feelings for me.

Before she's finished her orgasm, I settle between her legs, and my cock slides inside her contracting pussy.

Her eyes roll back, but I kiss her lips calmly as I stop after one thrust inside her. I'm going to move slowly, so she feels everything. I want her to have time to feel every emotion and articulate them before I have her losing her mind.

"Look at me," I say.

She takes her time, but eventually, her bright eyes are staring into mine.

I rock into her gently.

"You're mine."

She bites her lip at my words. I'm not sure she truly believes me.

"Say it."

"I'm yours."

I nod, kissing her again as I slide through her slick walls again.

"And you're mine," she says, unprompted.

Good girl.

I rub my thumb over her clit in slow circles.

"You're intoxicatingly beautiful."

"You're frustratingly handsome."

Yes, this is how I get her to say 'I love you.' She'll follow whatever I say, but can I tell her that I love her? Can I tell her and protect her at the same time?

My heart pounds wildly in my chest until I'm sure she can tell how nervous I am. I've never told a woman I loved her, but I know without a shadow of a doubt that I love Liesel. I always have; I've just been looking for any excuse that I can to not love her. Now, I can't stop loving her.

"You were the first person to have a nickname for me," I kiss her.

I rock into her as slowly as I can muster, trying to draw this out, but damn, is my cock obsessed with her. I won't last nearly as long as I want.

"You are the only person to ever have a nickname for me," she says against my lips.

I thrust harder.

"Only your kids could feel like mine."

"Only you could take care of my kids like they were your own."

More—more of everything.

"Only your fierceness could be enough to tame me."

"Only your strength could be enough to own me."

SO. FUCKING. CLOSE.

"I hate you," I kiss her, trying to hold our orgasms back for a couple more seconds.

"And I hate you." She nips at my bottom lip.

It's now or never.

Say it!

NOW.

"I—I lov—"

Her lips press against mine, hard.

Our tongues swarm each other. Our breaths combine. Our bodies slam together as we reach our climaxes.

We shake from the aftermath, tremble in each other's arms.

Our lips are still locked together, so I gently pull them apart.

I failed.

I didn't get her to say 'I love you,' and I didn't say it myself.

She smiles up at me, and the moment is over. Her brain is working again. If I say 'I love you' now, she'll just think I'm crazy, and she won't say it back.

I have to find a different way.

She's expecting the worst, not for me to tell her I love her.

She's prepared for the nightmare, not the dream.

I consider my options. Liesel is a stubborn woman who will refuse to admit her love for me. She's scared, and I'm not even sure she realizes what her feelings are for me. She says she's not capable of falling in love with anyone.

"What?" She frowns up at me, her eyes searching mine for what's going on in my head.

I lick my lips, trying to buy myself time, trying to think of another way—I can't. I've tried everything else. I promised I wouldn't hurt Liesel, but sometimes the only way to reveal the love in a person's heart is to cause their heart to bleed.

"I'm sorry," I say, knowing what I must do.

"Do your worst," she says, and then she kisses me hard on the lips.

Oh, huntress, you have no idea what my worst is. You call me killer for a reason. I'm about to murder your heart and hope that when you are picking up the pieces, you realize your true feelings.

24

LIESEL

We just made love.

That's what Langston was going for—a romantic night filled with hot, dirty sex. Then breakfast in bed, followed by slow lovemaking and a declaration of his love.

It was beautiful, magical. I could feel his love in every kiss, every touch, every breath.

He poured everything he had into showing me with his body just how much he loves me. I just couldn't let him do it with his words.

For years I've managed to keep him hating me for real. I just have to keep him from loving me for a little bit longer.

I told him to do his worst, so I'm preparing for it, even as his naked body still lies on top of mine. Even in the afterglow of what just passed between us, I know what comes next is going to hurt like a motherfucker. It's going to hurt worse than anything that happened to me in that game, on that yacht, when I was raped—all of it combined because Langston is going to be the one hurting me.

He thought it would make it easier on us if he said he loves me, easier to heal after he's done the terrible task he has to do for the treasure. We would be more connected if he said the words, but I know that's not true.

Words said or not; I've already fucked up. I already let us get too close. I'm just hoping that whatever way he has to torture me now will break both of our hearts enough that we can't possibly stay together.

For once, I hope my father came up with some wicked game to ruin us.

I run through all the things that Langston could do to prepare myself. If I could force my heart to break first, I'd do it, but I can't. Langston is the only one who has that power over me. And once he does destroy my heart, I have to be careful not to let either of our hearts break again.

Could he fuck another woman in front of me?

Could he break up with me, divorce me?

Take my kids away from me?

Physically hurt me? Rape me?

Each image plays in my head. I feel the pain; I feel my heart expanding in each instance, pushing it to its limits. I see it getting stabbed, ripped, cracked, but it never fully breaks.

Because I love him unconditionally; I love him wholly. Despite what he does, he's doing it to save our child, not because he wants to hurt me. There is nothing he can do that will make me stop loving him.

Fuck, if this is how I feel, I'm sure Langston feels the same. I don't know what it's going to take to get rid of our love, but I'm going to figure it out.

Langston closes his eyes as his body continues to pin me to the deck of the sailboat. When they open, there's a wicked fire. He's flipped a switch inside. Before, he was a man; now, he's the devil.

I purse my lips and try to breathe to control my heart-beat, not that I've been able to control my fucked up heart before. I already know I'm a goner. *Is dying by love a real thing that can happen?* If so, I'm going to die from loving Langston too much.

I'm rambling in my head, trying to process this moment to keep it separate from what happened earlier tonight. Maybe whatever Langston has to do will break him hard enough that he won't be able to be in the same room as me. He will stay away from me, and distance will make our love fade.

I bite my lip as he rubs himself against me.

Nope, I don't think there is anything that will make me stop loving him. The only way our love is dying is tragically, without the words ever being said out loud.

"Stop trying to guess what I'm going to do, huntress. You don't have a clue." The sinful gleam in his eyes tells me I don't.

He leans forward and whispers in my ear, "And to make sure you don't fuck up my plans, I'm going to tie you to the mast."

"You shouldn't have told me your plan."

"I didn't even tell you half of my plan."

"You told me enough." I squeeze my legs tight, trapping his junk before I knee him hard.

"Jesus," he groans as he rolls off me.

I grin and run.

I'm just delaying the inevitable, but I want him to do whatever he has to do with my arms and legs free. I don't think I can handle giving up so much control in my moment of torture.

There aren't many places to run on this boat. My choices are to jump overboard or head down into the below decks. I decide to head down, knowing he'll catch me if I jump into the water.

There are six steps down that lead down to a short

hallway and one door. I pop the door open and then throw it shut, slamming my body against the door as I flip the lock. I press my ear against the door, listening carefully.

I listen for his footsteps down the stairs or in the hallway, but I hear nothing.

Strange.

I hold my breath, thinking the sound of my breathing is affecting my ability to hear, but I still hear nothing. Then again, Langston can move silently.

I expect him to start kicking down the door any second now, but he doesn't.

He's messing with my head; I think, after twenty minutes have passed, and he hasn't made any attempt to come after me.

I slink to the floor and pull my knees to my chest as I continue to rest my ear against the door, waiting.

"Waiting for me?" Langston says from behind me.

I jump.

It's too late—Langston has me pinned to the door.

"How did you get in here?"

"I have to have some secrets," he winks at me as he growls and pins my hands above my head. My hips are trapped against the door with his.

"Don't even think about trying to knee me again."

He leans in close, and I bite at his lip. "How about if I bite?"

"I can handle the biting," he gruff.

Kiss me, I think.

Our naked bodies are pressed against each other, and even though we fucked all night and again this morning, I can't get enough. Maybe it's because I know our time is running out, or maybe it's because it's him.

He possesses my body as he breathes into me. His nostrils

flare—maybe in anger, or maybe in preparation for another attack.

I feel the familiar wetness drip between my legs. I can't believe I'm getting turned on from him manhandling me, even knowing that what he's doing now is just the tip of what's to come.

He steps back and yanks me away from the door before he kicks once hard against the door. The door falls easily. If only our hearts broke as easily.

He grabs my wrists, but I'm able to slip one out.

He pulls.

I pound on his back with my free fist and dig my heels into the ground, making it almost impossible for him to drag me out of the room.

He murmurs something in a gruff voice I can't make out.

Then he yanks me to him in one jolt.

I move my punches to his head, determined not to let him tie me up. If he wants to hurt me, he's going to have to do it while I'm free.

He shakes his head. "You'll never learn. You're mine, huntress. You hunt while I go in for the kill. Tonight, you're the one I kill."

He lets go of my wrist, and I know what he's going to do. It's too late, though. He's faster than me.

I try to run back into the room, but he grabs my calves and flips me over his shoulder.

"Langston! Put me down!"

I flail my arms, pounding into his back, his ass, anything I can reach. He doesn't let go. I dig my nails and teeth into his back, but no amount of pain that will make him put me down. He's decided how he wants to do this, and for some reason he thinks it will be easier if I'm tied up.

I have to think of another way.

I stop fighting, saving my energy as he carries me up the stairs.

The sun hits my back, and once again, I hear the waves of the ocean as the boat rocks gently. He's going to have to set me down to try and tie me up, so my only other choice is to jump into the ocean.

I take slow, deep breaths, trying to prepare my lungs for a long shot. If I can swim back to the island or to one of the other yachts, then maybe Langston will give up on trying to tie me up. He'll feel like we are running out of time and just get on with whatever horrible thing he has to do.

"If you are going to hurt me physically, you don't have to tie me up to do it. I can take it."

"I know," he says as he sets me down. By the tone of his voice, I know he's not going to change his mind. He still thinks he has to tie me up first.

So the second that my feet hit the ground again, I run as hard as I can in a straight line toward the side of the boat. I dive under the water, holding my breath for as long as I can. I pretend I'm a dolphin free in the ocean, even though I'm as far as you can get from being free.

I pop up finally when I run out of oxygen, but I can already feel Langston behind me. He knew what I was going to do.

He catches me in two strokes, wrapping his arms around me so I can't swim anymore. I'm relying on him completely to keep us above water.

He leans down and kisses me, sweeping me away. We're floating away in the ocean, away from all the heartbreak that awaits us.

He kisses me harder, his tongue rocking like the waves in my mouth. My heart thaws, my body relaxes. My mind tries to remind me of something, but I can't think why my brain would need to interrupt me right now.

And then I'm being hauled up. My body is no longer in the ocean, but my lips are still locked against Langston's as we both breathe hard into each other's mouths.

His eyes are filled with guilt. Finally, I feel it—the rope around my wrists. He's tied them together without me even realizing. He used his kisses as a weapon to control me, and I fell for it.

I swear I see a teardrop as he lifts my arms above my head and ties me to the pole.

"Killer," I plead in a whisper, but I stop fighting. He's already won.

He ties each of my ankles with a rope until they are spread apart.

My body reacts immediately, thinking that we are going to fuck instead of whatever horrible thing is going to happen next. My nipples pucker, wetness spreads between my legs, and my body heats.

He steps in front of me like he's trying to decide what he does next. He doesn't have any sort of weapon in his hand, which is a good sign, but I have no clues as to what dark sin he's about to commit.

"One more time," he brushes his lips against mine. "I just need you one more time first."

One more time until what?

I can't ask because his lips are against mine again, and his fingers are cupping my sex, spreading my wetness over my sensitive nub. I should keep my wits about me. After all, him kissing me last time was how I lost, but I don't care. I can't not kiss him, so I put everything into the kiss.

I don't know why Langston feels like this could be one of our last times, but he does, and I'm not going to let one time go to waste.

I can't move, being tied and naked to this pole, but it doesn't matter. Langston is the master of my body. He knows how to turn me on, how to bring me to the edge, how to slow me down, so I don't come too fast. He knows everything—even how to make me forget that I'm supposed to be fighting him, that I can't love him.

When he kisses my lips, I moan.

When he teases my nipples, I groan.

When he pinches my clit, I see stars.

"I could listen to the sound of you coming forever."

"You should."

He kisses me tenderly again, sucking on my bottom lip. "Maybe I'll keep you tied up naked forever, so I can always have my way with you, whenever I want you."

"Maybe," I say in a daze.

Then he steps back away from my body until the sun hits me in my face, reminding me that something sinister is about to happen.

I look at Langston standing naked in all his glory. His cock is hard, but he ignores it. He made me come, but he didn't fuck me. The one more time thing was about getting me riled up, giving me one more gift before he hurts me.

He walks over to a bag I didn't notice before. He digs inside with his back turned to me.

I hold my breath, waiting to find out my fate. *What horrible crime do we have to overcome?*

When he turns back to me, he's holding a knife.

I tense.

I can handle a knife, though. *Cut me, slice my skin, mark me. I'll still love you.*

Langston's eyes darken.

"I wish we had more time," he whispers.

"Me too," I whisper back.

My eyes look down, then up. "Do what you have to. Hurt me; I already forgive you."

"You won't forgive me for this."

He paces back and forth a second. He doesn't want to hurt me, just like I didn't want to hurt him, but we have to save Declan.

"Whatever it takes," I whisper.

His eyes meet mine again. They're dark orbs; I can't see any of the whites of his eyes. A hurricane of feelings roars in his eyes.

He could say it.

I love you.

I can't stop him. I can't shut him up with a kiss. I can't throw my hand over his mouth. I could try to talk over him, but he would still say it.

Suddenly, I'm panicking again. I struggle against the ropes, but they're bound so tightly. Langston himself taught me how to escape bindings, even his own, so I don't give up. I glance up, and I see a stray end of the rope. *Maybe if I can tug on it, I'll be able to get free?*

Langston says something, and it draws my attention back to him. He's twirling the knife around in his hand.

"The next location to find the treasure is Tokyo."

"Okay," I say. Now, stop stalling and do the thing so you can untie me, and we can get out of here.

"Tell the kids I love them," he says.

I frown, confused. "Sure, do you want me to stay here while you go? I don't think they'll let you get the treasure by yourself. I'm pretty sure I have to be there, too."

He shakes his head.

"I'm sorry," he says again.

"It's okay. Stab me or whatever, and then we can go."

That's when he turns the knife around and directs it toward his own heart.

"Langston….what are you doing?"

"Have Enzo cut out my heart. It's going to be too hard for

you to do it. Then take it to Tokyo. The exact address is in the bag."

"Langston, no!"

"I love you, huntress. I always have." Then he jabs the knife into his chest, directly into his heart.

He collapses to the floor, away from me.

"Langston!" I yell.

I wait, looking for any signs of life.

He groans.

He's still alive.

But then I see a puddle of blood on the ground underneath his body.

I can't tell if his chest is rising or falling.

"Langston!" I shriek again.

My yelling does nothing. This is why he tied me up. This is why he was so heartbroken. He knew he had to die, and he knew I would try to rescue him unless I was bound.

I reach for the rope that's hanging down. My fingertips just barely touch the bottom of the rope.

"Don't you dare die, Langston!" I yell through my tears. They're flowing uncontrollably down my face. I'm going to have to get used to the tears because if Langston is really dead, there is no way I'm ever going to be able to turn the tears off.

I cling to the end of the rope and pull with everything I can, but nothing happens. I try to jerk my wrists free, but somehow the ropes tighten. I can barely see through my tears.

"Help! Help!" I scream at the top of my lungs, knowing there are yachts nearby, but I don't see any headed our way.

I tug again, and again, trying to free myself. Nothing happens. I can't move.

"Langston!" I cry out again, desperate for him to get up,

for him to not die, but that's not my life. He's gone. I can sense it. He would do anything to save Declan, even die.

He just didn't think through the whole tying me to the mast, so I can't escape thing. Hopefully, he texted someone to come here, because if not, who knows how long it's going to be until someone comes to look for us.

My stomach flips, and I think I'm going to puke. My entire body trembles as saltwater sprays my face.

I want to collapse into a ball. I want to grab onto an anchor and drown myself, so I can be with Langston, but that's not fair. The kids need me if they can't have their father.

Tell them I love them.

Fuck you, Langston.

Fuck you.

I hate you.

I sob again, uncontrollably. A wail leaves my body that I'm sure rattles the entire earth in a massive, global earthquake.

I hate you so much, Langston.

I feel the ring on my finger.

He married me.

He protected me all the way to the end.

He *loved* me.

I take it back—hearing those words meant more to me than I realized. Hearing him actually speak the thing I've known all this time out loud proves that we should have been saying those words to each other since the first time we felt them, fuck the consequences and the broken heart. Knowing we've loved each other for years and not having said anything now that he's gone is ruining me.

"I love you, too," I whisper.

I squeeze my eyes shut as another heart-wrenching scream leaves my body. My heart is shattered. I will never love again. There is no way to repair the millions of pieces of my heart.

Say it again, Langston's voice says.

I open my eyes and see a hallucination. *Maybe it's his ghost already haunting me?*

Whatever it is, he's floating in front of me with a glow around him.

Say it again.

"I LOVE YOU!" I scream at the top of my lungs. "I've always loved you," my voice breaks. "Why did you leave me?" Then my voice leaves me; I open my mouth, and nothing else comes out.

"Only you would wait until I die to tell me you love me. But if death is the only way you'll tell me you love me, then so be it," Langston says.

My brain must have finally lost it because I'm pretty sure Langston is standing in front of me, very much alive.

"I'm going to kill you," I murmur as my heart finally beats again.

25

LANGSTON

I CHUCKLE through my own tears.

Hearing her shriek and cry over my fake death almost broke me. Lying on the ground, covered in fake blood, trying not to move was the hardest thing I've ever had to do. I've never heard such pain. It was like a pack of wolves tore into my own heart as I felt her heartbreak ooze off her, knowing that the only way to save her is to be patient and let her feel everything.

If my plan hadn't worked, I would have felt horrible forever. There would be no way that either of us would forgive me for causing her so much pain.

Thank god, it worked. She finally said the words, and she can't take them back.

Despite the agony we were both in, hearing her say she loves me was the most magical sound I've ever heard. I would die a thousand deaths if that is the only way I get to hear that she loves me.

Liesel's face is covered in tears, snot, and sweat. Her hair is matted to her head. Her body glistens with saltwater still clinging to her body. Or it might also be tears, snot, and sweat.

I'm not sure she has fully processed that I'm alive and not dead. I'm not a figment of her imagination; I faked my death.

I cup her face. "Huntress? Talk to me."

"No, get the hell away from me!"

She struggles with the ropes, trying to wiggle free. Seeing her naked body shimmy in front of me stirs my cock to life. Damn, do I want to fuck her senseless now that I've heard her admit that she loves me. Although I'm pretty sure when she gets free, she really will kill me given how angry she seems to be.

"I'm alive. It was all fake. I had to get you to admit you love me—"

"And pretending you were dead was the only idea you could come up with? You're a monster!"

I grab her face, and she jerks her head away.

"Untie me," she says.

I inhale her scent. "Not yet."

Her eyes shoot back at me with fire. "Untie. Me."

"Not until we finish talking. My task was to get you to admit you love me."

"I don't—"

"You do. You have this entire time, same as me, but you wouldn't admit it. I did a night of romance and a morning of lovemaking. We've already been through hell together, and you still wouldn't say the words out loud. Why? Why didn't you want to tell me?"

"Why didn't you?" she snaps back.

Touchè.

We stare each other down. I need to untie her and let her release her wrath, but I'm not ready just yet.

"How did you get the supplies? The knife? The fake blood?"

"That's what I was doing while you locked yourself in the bedroom. I had my team bring me Rose's toy knife and blood from her Halloween costume last year."

"What did she go as?"

"A prince who had just slain a dragon. The knife was her sword. Atlas went as the dragon."

Her lips lift in a smile at the mention of our kids. When she sees me notice, she immediately glares again.

"Untie me," Liesel tries again.

"I will, but first, say it again."

She shakes her head. "You've heard those words leave my mouth for the last time."

"No, I've heard them for the first of a million times. Say it again."

"No. I'll say it in front of the person who will give us the next clue, but that's it. I'm not letting you hear me say those words ever again after what you put me through."

"You can hate me all you want. You can punish me and make me pay for my tactics, but it worked. And you can't take it back now; I know how you feel. There is nothing to be afraid of anymore."

Her eyes drop in guilt, scared of some unknown fear. I consider telling her why I never wanted to admit to loving her, but it's my burden to bear.

I lean in close until our lips are just grazing each others. "I love you," I say against her lips.

My hands reach up to untie her. I can't be greedy and expect to hear those words again until we reach Tokyo.

"I love you," she says back.

I grin the widest smile I ever have before.

"I love you, you fucking bastard," she says.

That makes me grin more.

"Now, untie—"

I release her arms.

She gasps.

Her hands fall to her sides as I kneel down and untie each of her legs. Then I stand in front of her. We are both naked. I'm covered in fake red blood.

Tentatively, her hands reach out and touch my chest where I fake stabbed myself. Her fingertips roam over my body as if she still needs to confirm I'm really here and not dead. I let her explore my body. She runs her hands over my pecs, my abs, and then she dips lower.

I hold my hands at my side, letting her do whatever she wants with me. She should be able to do whatever she wants —I'm an asshole.

Her nails dig into my flesh.

I hiss but still don't move. "Whatever it takes, remember? I had to do whatever it took to ensure Declan's safety."

She nods, but she won't just let this go.

She grips my cock in her hands.

I freeze.

I want to stop her before she does something she regrets, like cutting off my cock or balls for hurting her, but I won't. I will endure whatever punishment she thinks I deserve.

She slides her hand roughly up and down my length.

I suck in a ragged breath. My body shudders in delight as her nails skim over my sensitive flesh, but I doubt what she has planned has anything to do with pleasure. I try to calm myself down, to get my cock to settle, but when she's touching me, there is nothing I can do that will stop me from getting hard.

She strokes me again.

I about come undone.

She smirks, enjoying the control she has over my body. Then she kneels—fucking kneels like the goddess she is.

"What are you doing?" I ask, too quickly.

"You don't get to ask me that after what you did."

She strokes my cock in her hands as she wraps her lips around the tip. Flashes of what she did to that poor guy on the sex-game yacht, where she practically bit off his cock come to mind. And I would deserve it if she did.

I try not to let myself enjoy it as she pushes her lips down my length. My cock hits the back of her throat, and she extends her tongue to lick my balls with the entirety of my shaft inside her mouth.

I hold back a groan and hold my breath waiting for her to turn vicious, but she just keeps sucking. Until I can barely stand, until my eyes roll back in my head, until I become dizzy with desire, she sucks. I can't hold back much longer.

Just when I'm starting to let my guard down, I feel my feet knocked out from underneath me.

I fall hard on my back.

Liesel climbs on top of me.

"I hate you," she growls as she straddles me.

"I know, but I'll never hate you again," I say.

She shakes her head stubbornly, and then she's pushing herself down on top of me. My cock sinks into her. She doesn't move initially; she just lets my cock stretch her.

Her eyes close, and a tear rolls down her cheek.

"Hey," I say, brushing her cheek. "I'm sorry. You're not going to lose me."

My words cause more tears, which makes me frown. I try to sit up. I'm not sure fucking is the right thing to do now, but then her hand is at my throat, and she's pushing me back down onto the floor. Her hips move over me hard. When she finally opens her eyes, there's a fierceness to them that shines through the tears.

She bounces on top of me, hard and fast. There isn't anything gentle about it—no long, loving strokes, caresses, sweet nothings. This isn't about lovemaking. This is her telling me how much she hates me.

I test the waters, meeting her thrust as she slams down on me. The look in her eyes turns more feral, so I take that as an affirmation that she wants me to fuck her, just as she's fucking me.

She pushes down harder on me, losing complete control in her thrusts. There is no way she's going to come if she keeps fucking me wildly like that.

Her grip on my throat loosens in her frustration, so I flip us over until I'm on top and in control.

I fuck her, slowing our strokes down so I can rub her clit and make her come.

She growls at my slower, more purposeful strokes. Her nails dig into my ass as she begs me to speed up. She leans forward and sucks my lip into her mouth, biting down hard.

I groan at the taste of blood in my mouth.

She pushes me hard in the chest, causing me to lose balance enough for her to roll us once again, so she's on top. I reach for her face, but she grabs my wrists and pins them overhead as her body fucks me furiously.

I could easily get out of her grasp, but the look in her eyes tells me if I try it, she will murder me—so I don't.

My hips meet hers thrust for thrust.

She arches her back, but her eyes stay locked on mine.

"I hate you," she spits out again.

"I love you," I say back.

Her eyes sparkle at my words like she's been waiting all this time to hear them, same as me. I'm pretty sure if I told her, 'I love you' enough, she would come from the sound of my voice alone.

"I love you, Liesel," I say as she drives her body down on me.

Her arms move down to my chest to get a better angle as she continues to fuck me, bruising our bodies with each thrust.

"I love you, huntress."

Her mouth falls open, her breathing faster. She's losing control, but she still spits out, "I hate you, killer."

I smile, loving her saying she hates me almost as much as I love hearing that she loves me. I just wish she would say the loving words easily and freely, that she didn't feel she has to keep them to herself.

My cock is drenched in her wetness, and I feel myself losing the fight to keep my orgasm back until she orgasms.

"Come, baby," I plead.

"Don't tell me what to do," she groans.

I try to move my hand to her clit to ensure she comes, but she swats my hand away.

"Liesel, I'm going to come. I need you to come with me."

She shakes her head, not stopping her movements. I'm not even sure if my words registered with her.

"Liesel, I—fuck!"

My dam bursts, and I come inside her.

Unexpectedly, she comes along with me.

I smile, my head falling back in complete exhaustion. There is no way to describe what we just did other than a hate fuck. But the fact that she did fuck me, instead of ignoring me or hurting me, says we can get past this. She won't hate me forever.

She falls against my chest, completely spent. Her hand strokes my chest where the fake blood is for a long time as the sun burns our bare skin.

"I love you," she whispers.

I close my eyes feeling those words stronger than ever. She loves me. I love her too. *What could tear us apart?*

"I love you, too."

LIESEL

I DON'T KNOW why I resisted saying 'I love you' for so long. Saying it even when I'm pissed at him is fucking incredible.

We lay in the sun, my head on his chest. As good as it feels, neither of us understands the danger that saying 'I love you' has caused; I can only guess.

Neither of us will take it back now, though.

The damage has been done, and our fates are set.

"We should get up and go have dinner with the kids before we take off," Langston says.

"Mmmh," I say, knowing he's right, but after thinking I lost him, I can't tear myself away from his body.

The anger at him faking his death returns; he put me through hell. I can't really be mad at him for long, though. He did it to get my stubborn ass to admit the truth and save Declan. Not to mention, I had Siren fake killed, and it almost destroyed him. Nonetheless, I let the anger fill me enough that I can unclench my claws from his body.

I sit up and smack him across the cheek. "Don't ever scare me like that again. I can't handle losing you."

He sits up, chuckling, and then crosses his heart like we are five again. "I promise."

"No more tricking each other. No more hiding. My heart can't take it."

"Neither can mine."

We kiss, but I don't let his tongue in my mouth. If we start that again, we will never leave this boat.

Langston scoops me up in his arms, then grabs his duffle bag before carrying me to the back of the boat.

"There are clothes in the bag to get dressed," he says as he sets me down and begins getting the sail back up.

I find yoga pants and an oversized shirt. I put them on and watch as Langston works, still completely naked.

Finally, he finishes his work and digs through the bag to find his own clothes.

"I think you need a bath before you get dressed. You have your guilt all over you," I say as annoyed as I can muster. Honestly, I'm just so happy that he's alive that I don't care he was the reason for thinking he was dead.

He shrugs a shirt on over the dried fake blood and pulls up his pants before sitting next to me. He doesn't speak as he kisses me on the forehead, but I know he's apologizing. He would spend the rest of his life apologizing if I let him. We both could.

That's not the life we want, though. I vow to myself that the second we step foot back on the island, I'm letting this shit go. I can't live my life mad at him forever.

Langston ties off the sailboat at the small dock on the island, and then he helps me off.

We start walking up the beach to the house. Our hands tangle together, and Langston looks at me.

I smile deliberately back. "I forgive you."

"What? You can't. I—"

"I forgive you. I love you." I kiss the back of his hand. "Now, let's go enjoy time with our family and friends."

I tug his hand, and he walks with me. I can tell he wants to talk about it more, but I'm not going to let us. Our time together is too precious.

Atlas and Rose see us as we approach the house. They run out and jump on us like we've been gone for months instead of just one day. That's what I regret the most—loving them, knowing the life we lead. There is always a chance we won't come back. A chance they will go through what I fake went through—losing Langston.

Langston frowns as I lift Atlas up into a hug. He seems to sense the turmoil going on in my head.

"Are you guys hungry?" Langston asks.

"Yes! I want pizza," Rose says.

"Me too," Atlas agrees.

"What are Uncle Enzo and Aunt Kai fixing?" Langston asks, assuming they are the ones doing the cooking.

"Pizza!" Rose yells.

We all laugh as we carry them inside. We stop in the kitchen and see that Enzo and Kai are, in fact, making pizza.

Cayden cries in Zeke's arms; both Atlas and Rose turn concerned. "We need to go cheer up baby Cayden. He cries if we aren't around him," Rose says.

Atlas nods.

We put both kids down, and they race over to Zeke to have a look at baby Cayden. To our surprise, Zeke lowers him to let him get a look at Atlas and Rose, and Cayden seems to stop crying. He reaches out to Atlas and touches his face.

But then I frown when I realize that Zeke can't hear any of the exchange the kids are having. He can't hear, and it's all my fault.

"It's not your fault," Beckett says from behind us.

Langston and I turn around. Langston is gripping my hand again.

Beckett walks closer and holds out his bandaged hand. "The doctors you sent took a look at all of us. Because you got us medical help so quickly, we are all going to heal; good as new."

I frown. That's not possible. Nothing is as good as new.

"Zeke's hearing has already started coming back. The doctors are extremely hopeful he'll get his hearing back completely within the year. If not, they can fit him with hearing aids that will get him to one hundred percent."

I look at Zeke in surprise.

"My hearing is already coming back," Zeke says. He either heard part of the conversation or guessed what we were talking about.

I nod, giving him a small smile.

"The doctors looked at Siren's vocal cords, and they're mostly infected at this point, not really damaged. It's painful, but Siren can already make small sounds. She's on painkillers and antibiotics, so she should heal quickly and be able to talk. Singing might take longer to come back, but it will return."

I stare down at his heavily bandaged hand. "And what about you? You lost the most. Without the ability to use your hand, life is going to be hard—way harder than it should be."

Beckett smirks. "I've lost a hand before. The body is amazing at adapting. If I lost this hand, too, I'd learn how to use the residual limb or my toes. The doctors gave me a salve to apply to the burns, though. I should heal, but if I don't, it's mostly cosmetic. My fingers still function even if I can't feel what I'm touching."

I wrap my arms around him. "It's still too high a price to pay."

"I just wish I had been able to save Declan," Beckett says.

I pull away from him and pat him on the shoulder.

"You're going to get the treasure to use to get Declan back, aren't you?" he asks.

Langston and I nod. "Let me go with you," Beckett pleads.

"No, you need to stay and watch the kids."

"Yea, cause I was so good at it the last time."

Atlas runs over to Beckett at that moment. "Come help make the pizzas. Uncle Enzo doesn't know what he's doing and is going to burn it."

Beckett nods and starts to follow Atlas.

"I think you do more than just 'good' with the kids. You're great and will do everything in your power to protect them. Stop blaming yourself," I say.

He heads into the kitchen after Atlas but stops just short. "You too."

I nod silently.

"I'm going to go check and make sure they know how to use the pizza oven, you okay?" Langston asks.

"Yep, go."

Langston reluctantly leaves my side and grabs one of the pizzas on the kitchen counter. He heads outside to the pizza oven on the far side of the deck with Atlas and Beckett in tow.

My stomach rumbles at the sight of the food, and a wave of nausea pulses through me. I race to the bathroom, thankful that Langston isn't nearby to question me.

I try to hurry in the bathroom, quickly rinsing my mouth out with mouthwash. When I open the door, I find Siren standing in the doorway.

Her eyes search mine, and I know she heard me puking my guts in the bathroom.

She rests her hand on my stomach with a knowing twinkle in her eye as she raises her eyebrows in question.

"No, just sick," I say, answering her question.

She frowns and moves her hand to my forehead. I'm sure it's hot and sweaty from being sick.

"I'm okay, just an upset stomach with everything going on. I'll be better once we get Declan."

She nods.

"Can you do me a favor?"

She tilts her head waiting for me to ask my question.

"Can you get Phoenix brought here to the island? Langston and I are leaving tonight, and although the kids are getting to know all of you, they trust her. She loves them, and she deserves a chance to say goodbye."

Siren frowns. It's not fair to ask her to do something like this when she can't really argue back. She can only either say yes or no.

The look on her face tells me she's going to say no, but she eventually nods.

"Thank you," I say as she pulls out her phone to text.

I'm not afraid of Phoenix hurting the kids again. There will be more people here this time to watch her. She already knows we have suffered and paid for causing her to lose her kids. Once she sees them again, she'll want to spend time with them. She won't hurt them. She loves them.

And the kids need as many parents as they can get, as many people who love them as possible. You never know when one of us might be taken away from them.

LANGSTON

"Mom!" the kids yell and jump up from their seats around the fire pit. They toss their empty plates to the side as they run down the beach.

For a second, I thought they were talking about Liesel, but then I turn and see Phoenix running up the beach.

She kneels down and hugs each of them. Her hugs and smiles seem genuine, but I know the wickedness that lies underneath.

My blood boils that she's near the kids.

I stand up and start storming down the beach to Phoenix with Liesel hot on my heels.

"Langston," Liesel warns from behind me. I snap my head to her, knowing she's the reason Phoenix is here.

"They love her. She loves them. We can't keep them apart; it's not fair."

I growl and then start down the beach again without speaking to Liesel. She continues to follow after me, I assume, to make sure I don't do anything stupid.

"Mom, have you met our other mom?" Rose asks Phoenix.

"I have. She's pretty awesome, isn't she?" Phoenix asks Rose.

"She is! I'm so excited. I get two moms! How lucky are we?" Rose grabs Atlas' hands and jumps up and down. He just rolls his eyes at her.

Phoenix stands and nods a thank you to Liesel before she turns to look at me. Without looking at the kids, I say, "Atlas, Rose, how about you race back to the house?"

"Are you going to race us?" Atlas asks.

"Us adults will race after you."

The kids take off.

I stare Phoenix down. "I'm doing this for them, not for you."

"Of course," Phoenix answers.

"If you hurt them, try to take them away again, do anything—I will kill you, your brothers, and anyone you've ever met. Do you understand?"

"I won't hurt them. I would never hurt them."

"You hurt them when you took them away from me, their father!"

"I'm sorry."

"Just say goodbye to them," I say.

Phoenix walks toward the house, and then it's just Liesel and me. We exchange glances but not words. I can't believe that Liesel trusts Phoenix. Trusting other people is what got us into this mess.

"Let's go say goodbye to the kids before we head to Tokyo," Liesel finally speaks instead of arguing with me.

I nod.

———

The plane ride to Tokyo is long, but I enjoy every minute of it.

We alternate between fucking and sleeping naked in each other's arms.

The car ride is more nerve-wracking as we think about what we are about to face. We pull up at the address and step out of the car.

The small temple sits on the edge of a river, covered in moss, bushes, and trees. The walls of the temple are barely visible through the overgrowth.

We approach the entrance and knock softly on the door.

A woman opens the door.

"I've been expecting you." She opens the door, and we enter. In retrospect, the tasks we've been given so far to prove we love each other were pretty easy. I shouldn't be upset with her father for this wild goose chase, but I am. I don't know what games he's playing from beyond the dead. If he weren't dead already, I'd kill him myself.

The room we enter is simple. You can see the beams holding up the roof, and there is a small, low to the ground, circular table with four small chairs around it.

"Sit, sit," the woman says.

We both take a seat at the table. The woman leaves the room, leaving Liesel and me alone. We both smile at each other, knowing this is almost over.

"Don't move," the woman suddenly says.

We both freeze, not sure what the hell is going on.

My eyes scan the room and find the woman has a gun pointed at my head. She's across the room, so I can't just yank the gun free from her hand. I have no idea how good her aim is.

"Do you love him?" she asks Liesel.

Liesel is sitting next to me with big eyes. I can hear her heart beating from here. After what I put her through, I know she's not going to let this woman shoot me without a fight.

"Yes, I love him," Liesel says.

"Would you die for him?" the woman asks.

"Yes," Liesel says at the same time I scream, "No!"

The woman turns the gun on Liesel. "If either of you moves, I'll kill her."

I freeze, even though I want to protect Liesel with every ounce of my being. I rock my feet under the table, preparing myself to jump on Liesel to protect her from any bullets if I need to.

"Do you love her?" she asks me.

"Yes, with everything I have," I say.

"Would you die for her?"

"In a heartbeat."

"No," Liesel says with tears in her eyes. She quickly wipes them away. I'm guessing the only reason she's not bawling right now is that she knows she has to remain strong for whatever happens next. She's going to need her sight to be able to fight or run.

The woman shakes her head at us.

"She loves me, and I love her. If you want us to prove it, we will. You don't need to kill either of us," I say.

The woman laughs. "You think you completed the task successfully?"

"Yes, I did what was on the card. I made her fall in love with me. Liesel loves me, and I love her."

"That was what was on the card, but that was not the actual challenge. Your task was to resist falling in love. You were told years ago what would happen if you fell in love with Liesel, now you will pay the price," the woman says.

Shit.

"What is she talking about?" Liesel asks.

I should have told Liesel, but I didn't want her to worry. Her father's dead; I didn't think he'd know or have any way to carry out his threat. I guess I was wrong.

"Go on, you can tell her, we have time," the woman says.

I should be figuring out how to get out of here, not tell Liesel a story about how horrible her father is. She already knows that, so I try my best to search for ways I can get Liesel out of here safely while I tell her the story.

"Your father saw us rip his letter to you in half. He knew you had half the clues, and I had the other half. So he looked me up, found out that I worked for Enzo Black, the son of one of his rivals who betrayed him. He approached me. It took me a minute to realize who he was, or I wouldn't have taken the meeting. He threatened me."

Actually, his men beat me to within an inch of my life.

"He told me he'd rather his daughter be dead than loved by a man like me. He saw already how much I wanted you, how I loved you. He made me promise before he'd let me go that I would never fall in love with you or let you fall in love with me. If I did, he'd kill one or both of us. At the time, I knew you hated me and didn't think you could ever love me, so I didn't see the problem with making that promise. I fell in love with you, anyway. I'm sorry for the danger it's put us in."

Her father was a snake. He set up this game and ensured that we failed. The only way she would have had a chance to win is if she had chosen someone else to marry.

"Your father left very clear instructions, Liesel. If you fell in love with Langston, then only one of you survives. Only one of you will be walking out of this temple alive. It doesn't matter which one of you it is. Either the two of you decide, or I do," the woman says.

I've found all the exits in this room. It's one woman against the two of us. I have a gun in the band of my pants. I just have to reach for it and shoot her dead faster than she can pull the trigger. More importantly, I have to ensure that Liesel doesn't get shot.

Liesel seems to be trying to read my mind as I plan out our escape. I don't know if she gets the message or agrees with it, but when I whisper, "Now." Liesel takes the hint and dives as hard as she can underneath the table.

I dive after her as I grab my gun and aim at the woman.

I fire.

The woman fires.

"You okay?" I ask Liesel.

She nods.

"We have to get out of here. Crawl behind me toward that back door. Understood?" I ask.

She nods.

I fire rapidly in the direction of the woman as Liesel starts crawling. I use my body to shield her, but the woman hasn't fired at us since I aimed my gun at her. She seems to be hiding behind the wall.

"Go!" I yell.

Liesel runs; I run after her.

We throw open the back door, exit, and find ourselves on a garden terrace.

It's eerily quiet out here. We have to trek around the temple to get to our car. I don't spot the woman who was shooting at us, and I don't know if she has anyone else working for her, so I keep Liesel behind me as I hold out my gun, and we start creeping around the outside of the temple.

We don't make it a step before we are being fired upon. We duck down behind a pillar as I return fire.

"Oh my god," Liesel says as she catches a quick glance of the garden before she hides behind the pillar.

My eyes scan the garden. There are at least thirty men approaching us in tactical gear.

Fuck.

"We need to get back in the temple."

"We can't. They have us surrounded. There are men coming out of the temple now."

I glance behind us and see she's right—more men storm out of the temple.

I have a gun with limited bullets. I don't think Liesel even has a gun. We have no backup team coming to rescue us. It's just the two of us, and as good as I am, I can't take down this many men. We need a miracle.

And if someone has to die, it's going to be me, not her.

LIESEL

THERE ARE SO many guns pointed in our direction right now. We are crouched behind a pillar. Langston has a gun with a limited number of bullets left. I don't see a way out of this.

And yet, all I can think about is how much of an asshole my father was. It would've been terrible enough for the fact that he wasn't around for most of my life. He ran a criminal organization and destroyed other people's lives. And instead of simply letting me inherit whatever this treasure is, he created an elaborate game that I have no chance of winning.

My father wanted me dead.

He didn't have the balls to do it himself, though. So he invented this game to ensure my death, but not after he thoroughly tortured me first.

Hiding the treasure had nothing to do with love, as he said in his letter. That story about him and my mother breaking up because the sheer quantity of the treasure sprouted greed was made up. They got divorced because he was a criminal, and my mother was an addict.

This is about control. My father wanted to control me even from death. He didn't want to give me any money unless I earned it. He wanted to choose who I married, who I loved. He thought Langston was unworthy.

I look to the man crouched next to me, protecting me, knowing that he'll probably die doing it. We could have loved each other so much sooner if my father hadn't intervened. I have no doubt the reason why Langston tried so hard to hate me all these years is to save me. Loving me was dangerous.

I understand now why he was so hesitant to say the words. Not because he didn't love me, but because he was afraid of getting one of us killed. I'm not going to let that happen. I just have to figure out what my dad's endgame was.

Is this it? Is this where he expected us to die? He set a trap for us, letting us get so close to the end only to kill us instead?

Maybe, but it doesn't make sense to me.

I rack my brain through all of the clues. I try to think of my father as the monster he is. The only monster I knew to be similar was Enzo's dad. He, too, set up ridiculous games in order for his son to inherit his company. He, too, tried to control his son's life.

This is no different. I just have to outsmart my father.

I'm beginning to think there isn't even a treasure to be found. *Then how are all these people getting paid? Why are they still loyal to my father after he's dead?*

There has to be a treasure. But what is it? Why hide it? Is it a reward or a way to punish me further?

My father was an evil man, so I lean toward punishment.

Suddenly it hits me all at once; I know what the treasure is! Still, it doesn't help me figure out how to get out of this mess alive.

I grab Langston's bicep. "Don't you dare sacrifice yourself. You saw what happened the last time I thought you died; I died right along with you. Don't sacrifice yourself."

Langston takes a deep breath. "I won't let you die. I have to protect you."

"No, you've done that, and this is where we've ended up. Whatever happens next, we do it together."

He nods.

"Promise me," I demand.

"Only if you promise the same."

"I promise," we both say at the same time, looking into each other's eyes. I can't lose him, and he can't lose me. We have no other option than to live or die together.

"What ideas do you have for getting out of here?" I ask.

"Not many. We are obviously outnumbered, so we have two options left, really. We try to fight our way out and get shot and killed, or we surrender and hope that gives us enough time to find another way out while they decide what to do with us."

"I don't love either of those options."

"I don't either."

"We surrender together. We call their bluff," I say.

"You don't think they'll actually kill us?"

"No, I think they will, but they will want to play with us first. They'll torture us until the brink of death and then kill us. We can both survive the pain. That gives Kai, Enzo, Siren, Zeke, Beckett—any of them—time to come save us. Or as you said, it gives us time to come up with a better way to escape or convince them to let us go."

His lips meet mine in the briefest of kisses, but his kiss tells me everything I need to know. Then his lips say it, "I love you, huntress."

"I love you, killer."

He grabs my hand, interlocking our fingers, and then we both stand with our hands up. Langston makes a show of dropping his gun.

"We surrender!" we both shout over the gunfire and yelling in our direction.

The gunfire almost immediately stops. The muffled shouts draw quieter.

"Don't move!" someone yells at us.

We don't. We feel two guns pressed against our backs, our arms are yanked behind our bodies, and our wrists are tied together with rope. Our eyes meet in a show of solidarity. If his eyes are the last thing I see before I die, I'll die having loved and been loved, which is more than I ever expected out of my life.

The men shove us into the center of the terrace until we are surrounded by the entire squad pointing guns at us.

I glance at Langston, realizing we might have chosen the wrong course of action to get us out of here. This doesn't feel like they are about to torture us. It feels like we're facing a firing squad.

The woman from inside comes out with a smirk on her face.

"Have you decided?" she asks.

When we don't answer, she tries again. "Have you decided which of you is going to die and which is going to live? Only one of you has to die; the other gets to live a long, happy life."

Langston looks at me, and I know it breaks him to not try and save me, but I shake my head, and he nods. We are star crossed lovers destined to die together.

"Either both of us live, or both of us die; there is no other option," I say.

The woman smiles. "Fine, it makes no difference to me. I get paid either way."

"Look at me," Langston says.

I turn my head and stare deeply into his eyes.

This is the moment when it all ends; we die.

I should be terrified.

Shaking.

Crying.

Begging.

I should be afraid of death. I'm not.

I smile. Langston smiles back.

We love each other. I have no regrets. If I only got to love Langston out loud for a day, it was enough. We got our one day. That's more than most people experience after a lifetime of searching. Our love was real; it was all-encompassing. It was enough.

"Fire!" she screams.

I hold onto Langston's eyes for as long as I can, but eventually, the hits of the bullets are going to knock me dead. I hold onto his eyes until the darkness comes.

The darkness comes too soon; Langston is gone, and I'm in hell.

LANGSTON

D*YING—WHAT does it feel like?*

Immense nothingness.

The darkest of darks.

I didn't feel any pain, which shocks me. Death should be the worst pain, but all it feels like is a final end—an eternal end, an erasing of memories.

And yet, I remember her—Liesel, my huntress.

I may have forgotten everything else, but her love can't be taken from me, not even by death.

My mind clings to the memory of Liesel.

Where is she? Is she dead too? Is she floating in this darkness with me?

I dip down, my stomach drops.

How is that possible?

Am I an angel? Am I flying?

Voices register in my brain.

What is that?

I move my fingers. *I still have fingers!* They barely operate at first, but the more I wiggle, the more control I have over them.

Finally, I'm able to move them enough to feel my face. There is fabric covering my head. I push it up, and light blinds me. I try to close my eyes, but my lids move too slowly. Everything moves too slowly.

I'm not dead.

I'm on an airplane, by the looks of it.

Liesel is sitting down the aisle from me in a chair facing Corbin and Maxwell. She's not dead, either. She's very much alive.

Did they save us?

"Why did you save us?" Liesel asks them.

"You know why," Corbin answers.

Maxwell looks annoyed and tired by this conversation, like they've already been talking for a long time.

She frowns. "The treasure."

Corbin nods.

Liesel considers. "I'll find the treasure, just leave my kids alone."

Corbin smiles; it's what he wants.

"No!" I say, but nothing comes out. They don't look at me. *Am I really here? Maybe I am dead?*

"You will help me find the treasure; otherwise I'll kill you and Langston, and all three of your children will grow up parentless. But first, I need proof that you've paid your sacrifice. I saw Beckett's hands. Maxwell saw Siren and Zeke's sacrifices. None of us were there to witness your sacrifice, however," Corbin says.

"How do I prove it?" Liesel frowns.

"We'll go to a hospital to get an ultrasound."

Ultrasound? Do they think she's pregnant too?

"That's a waste of time. We need to go, now," she insists.

"You need to pay your dues first."

"Do you have a knife on you?"

Corbin frowns and looks at Maxwell, who reluctantly

pulls out a knife. She snatches it from their hands, and then I watch in horror as she lifts up her shirt and plunges the knife into her lower belly.

"No!" I try to scream again. I try to kick, to fight, but in my drugged-up state, I can't do any of those things.

She removes the knife, then takes off her shirt until she's just in a bra and wraps it around her fresh wound. "Does that satisfy you? I sacrificed my ability to get pregnant. I injected the poison you gave me at the club, and I just stabbed myself in the uterus. There is no way I'll ever be able to get pregnant."

Corbin grins, pleased.

"That will do."

My stomach twists, aching to go strangle the man to death.

Liesel speaks again. "Now I want something first. Take Langston back to his private island and ensure he gets medical help right away. Don't hurt him or my kids ever again."

"Very well. Maxwell, take Langston to his island and see that he gets medical help. Assure him that we won't hurt or take his kids from him ever again."

I lose consciousness. The next time I awake. I'm on a new plane, alone with Maxwell.

"Don't worry, Corbin won't kill Liesel," Maxwell says. "He won't kill her."

The darkness pulls me under once again.

LIESEL

NOW THAT LANGSTON, Rose, and Atlas are all safe, I'm able to focus on what comes next.

"What happens when we find the treasure?" I ask.

"You've realized that Langston isn't going to be able to help you get the treasure on his own. The way your father set up the game was to make sure you'd fail if you chose to find it with him."

"Yes, I realize that," I say.

Corbin sips his whiskey. "Good, so let's talk. I want the treasure. You'll help me get it, and then I'll let you go free. You'll be free to live your life with the man you love and two gorgeous children."

My heart sinks thinking about what that life would be, but it doesn't matter. That would never be my life, no matter if Corbin intervened or not.

"No."

Corbin frowns.

"Take me instead. Langston gets the treasure; you get me."

He looks at me slowly. "You figured it out, didn't you?"

I nod.

"Tell me," he says.

"In my father's story, the one with my mother, I was the treasure—the treasure that ruined their marriage, the treasure that wasn't worth it. The treasure isn't money or jewels. The treasure is a child, my child. The treasure is Declan."

Corbin nods for me to continue.

"You never had Declan. You tricked me into thinking you did so I would go after the treasure for you. You just want to hurt me. You want to take all of my kids away from me so I'll feel the pain Phoenix went through. The pain you all went through because of my father."

"Very good. So you see, I can't give Langston the treasure. I already caved to Phoenix and Maxwell, who both have big hearts and wanted me to give you the kids back. I won't cave when it comes to Declan. We find him; I keep him. You go free and unharmed to return to what remains of your family —that's the deal."

I shake my head. It's a horrible deal. It means I'm trading one kid for the other two. I can't do that.

"No, take me instead. Take me and give Declan to Langston. You want to hurt me? This is how you do it. You separate me from all of my kids, not just one. You separate me from the man I love."

Corbin doesn't want to kill me; that would be too easy. He just wants me to suffer as his family did and continues to suffer to this day.

Corbin considers my proposition for a minute. For several long seconds, he doesn't speak. He just sips his drink, thinking it over and looking at me. I don't know what I'm going to do if this doesn't work. What other options do I have?

This has to work.

"I know your secret," he finally says.

I freeze.

"How?"

"It doesn't matter. What matters is that I do know, so I also know your deal is not a fair trade."

I understand what he's saying, but it's all I have to offer—my life for Declan's. I was put on this earth to save my family. I'm not going to fail at my one mission.

"All you've ever wanted to do is make me pay for the atrocities of my father. Take the deal. Me for Declan."

More time passes. He considers his options. I consider mine.

"If you don't take this deal, then you get no deal. You don't find Declan without me. He stays hidden forever. This is the only way you get what you want."

Another second passes before he holds out his hand.

"Deal."

———

Thank you so much for reading Dangerous Lies! Langston & Liesel's story concludes in Endless Lies

One-click ENDLESS LIES now >

"AMAZING! Talk about edge of your seat suspenseful, non-put-down-able, emotional and gut wrenching book. WOW, just WOW!" —Reviewer

JOIN ELLA's NEWSLETTER & NEVER MISS A SALE OR NEW RELEASE → ellamiles.com/freebooks

Haven't read **Enzo and Kai's story** yet?
I should have run away, found a new life, and started over.
Instead, I returned.
To find the man who sold me.
One-click Taken by Lies for FREE >

Haven't read **Zeke and Siren's story** yet?
She saved me. And now, seeing her about to be sold to the highest bidder, it's my turn to save her.

Stolen by Truths #4

Possessed by Lies #5

Consumed by Truths #6

DIRTY SERIES:

Dirty Obsession

Dirty Addiction

Dirty Revenge

Dirty: The Complete Series

ALIGNED SERIES:

Aligned: Volume 1 (Free Series Starter)

Aligned: Volume 2

Aligned: Volume 3

Aligned: Volume 4

Aligned: The Complete Series Boxset

UNFORGIVABLE SERIES:

Heart of a Thief

Heart of a Liar

Heart of a Prick

Unforgivable: The Complete Series Boxset

ABOUT THE AUTHOR

Ella Miles writes steamy romance, including everything from dark suspense romance that will leave you on the edge of your seat to contemporary romance that will leave you laughing out loud or crying. Most importantly, she wants you to feel everything her characters feel as you read.

Ella is currently living her own happily ever after near the Rocky Mountains with her high school sweetheart husband. Her heart is also taken by her goofy five year old black lab who is scared of everything, including her own shadow.

Ella is a USA Today Bestselling Author & Top 50 Bestselling Author.

Stalk Ella at:
www.ellamiles.com
ella@ellamiles.com

www.ingramcontent.com/pod-product-compliance
Lightning Source LLC
Chambersburg PA
CBHW021141190726
48288CB00008B/2762